**Virginia McEnery**—All she wants for Christmas is a mommy. Trouble is, Amanda, the mommy she's chosen, doesn't think she's right for the job. But maybe with a miracle—and a little help from Santa—Virginia can change Amanda's mind....

**Amanda Donnelly**—Her co-workers call her Scroogette...because she hates Christmas. She's not wild about kids, either. Then she's assigned to do a TV story on kids *and* Christmas. Isn't life wonderful? When Virginia turns out to be a terrific little girl, things begin to look up. If only Virginia's father wasn't so delightfully disturbing...

**Kirk McEnery**—He doesn't need any more complications in his life. Especially not this close to Christmas. Then he starts to realize that Amanda might be the kind of complication he could get really interested in....

Dear Reader,

Kids and Christmas just go together, don't they? I'll confess that we still believe in Santa Claus at my house. Just a couple of days ago, my younger son asked if there really is a Santa Claus. I could tell he hoped I'd say yes, and so I hesitated.

"Last year at the mall, Santa knew my name and I didn't have to tell him," he reminded me. Well, yes, but I can explain that.

"And what about the time I dropped Randy Raccoon and Santa knew *his* name?" Now, I *can't* explain that.

I tried out the "Santa represents the magic of Christmas" line. My son replied, "But is he a real person? Can we fax him?"

"Fax Santa Claus?" I stared into my son's hopeful face and heard myself say, "We can try."

"Will he fax back?"

"Probably just a form acknowledgment. He's busy this time of year."

My son grinned. "If Santa's got a fax machine, then he's got to be real."

And so Santa will be visiting our house one more time. Electronically.

Merry Christmas!

*Heather Allison*

# THE SANTA
# SLEUTH
## Heather Allison

# *Harlequin Books*

TORONTO • NEW YORK • LONDON
AMSTERDAM • PARIS • SYDNEY • HAMBURG
STOCKHOLM • ATHENS • TOKYO • MILAN
MADRID • WARSAW • BUDAPEST • AUCKLAND

For True Believers everywhere

Especially
Brett and Collin MacAllister
Daniel, Andrea and Adam MacAllister
and Laura Shin

Special thanks and Merry Christmas to Elizabeth Wiggs,
Marilyn Amann, Pat Kay, Carla Luan,
Alaina Richardson and Sue Royer

ISBN 0-373-03341-9

THE SANTA SLEUTH

# CHAPTER ONE

"DO YOU BELIEVE in Santa Claus?"

Amanda Donnelly squatted to half her height and stared intently into the freckled face of a small boy. He stared back. "Do you believe in Santa Claus?" she repeated a bit impatiently. Honestly, finding a child to feature as a Santa Sleuth in her story was harder than she'd thought.

The boy, cute, but not vocal, nodded, then looked up at his kindergarten teacher for approval. She patted him on the shoulder and raised her brows at Amanda.

With a slight shake of her head, Amanda straightened and met the principal's eyes.

"Thanks, Stephen," the teacher murmured, and sent the boy back to the classroom.

"Ms. Donnelly," said the elementary school principal, "have you made your decision?"

Amanda shook her head. "I need a child with more . . . *presence*. Not quite so babyish."

The teacher sent her an exasperated look. "Try first or second grade," she said, lowering her voice to a whisper and stepping back into her classroom. "Any older and they don't, you know, *believe*," she mouthed.

Amanda sighed. The executive producer at "Hello Houston," the popular local television show, was always getting clever ideas and assigning others to work out the details. Amanda had been assigned this story—a cute seasonal piece of fluff.

Amanda didn't want this story. She didn't particularly like working with children. She didn't like fluff pieces, and she loathed Christmas.

The executive producer, Kay, knew this, of course, and obviously thought the assignment might instill a little Christmas cheer in Amanda.

But it would take more than candy canes and red velvet to bring on the Christmas spirit.

"They lose their teeth in first grade, don't they?" Amanda asked the principal. "Could we find a precocious child who still has teeth?"

"Ms. Donnelly, this is a school, not a casting agency," Mrs. Hull chided as she led Amanda down the hall to the first-grade wing.

"I realize that," Amanda murmured, trying to mend fences. "And we do want that fresh unaffected quality professional child actors lack."

Professional child actors would have to be paid, and "Hello Houston" wanted to avoid talent costs on this segment. Amanda smiled with all the fake sincerity she could muster.

"I see." Mrs. Hull eyed her for a moment, then left her standing in the hallway and sailed into one of the classrooms.

Amanda was afraid the principal saw a great deal more than she should.

Leaning against the cool tile wall, Amanda sighed again. There it was, the school smell—a mix of pencils, paper and starchy lunches. A few feet away, two teacher's aides pulled Thanksgiving decorations from a bulletin board.

The Christmas season had officially arrived. Not that it mattered to her, except that the traffic around the malls would be impossible for weeks. Amanda always avoided it by ordering from catalogs. No muss, no fuss.

Mrs. Hull returned, five children trailing behind her, reminding Amanda of a large duck with her ducklings. Three boys and two girls lined up against the wall.

"Perhaps I could see the entire class?" Amanda suggested.

"These are the only ones with all their teeth," the principal said, showing hers.

Amanda knew she had to select one of these children or find another school. Mrs. Hull had only cooperated because Amanda promised that the school would be named on "Hello Houston." Principals were quite competitive, she'd discovered to her surprise.

"Are we in trouble?" asked one of the boys.

"No, Jason, not this time," Mrs. Hull reassured him.

Amanda mentally crossed him off her list. After talking with the children for a few moments, Amanda mentally crossed them *all* off her list. She wanted to cross the whole idea off her list.

"I'm sorry we couldn't be of any help to you," said Mrs. Hull, her feathers clearly ruffled.

As the principal thanked the first-grade teacher, Amanda looked over their shoulders and scanned the fidgeting class. Her attention was immediately caught by a pair of steady blue eyes, staring out from the face of an angel. The angel had hair of spun-gold ringlets.

Perfect.

"Could I talk to that little girl?" Amanda asked, pointing into the classroom.

"She's missing a front tooth," replied the principal.

"Only one?"

"As far as I know."

Amanda ignored the principal's tone. "Please?"

For a moment Mrs. Hull looked as though she'd refuse, but then she capitulated.

The little girl and her teacher came out into the hallway, but noise from the rest of the students drew the teacher back inside.

"Hi," Amanda said, slightly disconcerted by the child's direct gaze. "Do you believe in Santa Claus?"

"Maybe," the girl replied, and tilted her head. "Will I get a Super Nintendo if I do?"

Amanda blinked.

"Virginia!" said the shocked principal.

"Her name's Virginia?" Amanda turned to the principal, who nodded.

"Oh—" Amanda looked heavenward "—it's a sign. Yes, Virginia, there is a Santa Claus. And we're going to find him." Amanda fumbled in her purse for a business card.

"Where are we going to find Santa?" Virginia asked.

"At the mall, honey." Amanda thrust a card at the teacher, who stood within earshot, then one each to the principal and Virginia.

"I don't read very good yet." Virginia tried to sound out "Amanda."

"It says my name, Amanda Donnelly, and that I'm an associate producer with 'Hello Houston.' Have you ever watched 'Hello Houston' on TV?"

Virginia wrinkled her nose. "Is it a cartoon?"

"Sometimes." Amanda grinned.

Virginia grinned back. The missing tooth wasn't so bad. In fact, it was kind of cute.

Mrs. Hull stepped to the classroom door, where she and the teacher engaged in a whispered conference.

"Excuse me." The teacher motioned Amanda toward her. With cautionary looks at Virginia, they moved several yards down the hall.

"You don't want to work with Virginia," warned the teacher.

Amanda took great exception to being told what she did or did not want. "She's perfect. Cute, personable, quick thinking for a kid, and I was wrong about the teeth."

"Oh, she's smart. Very smart. But..." The teacher darted a glance at the principal.

"We feel another child might better represent Cameron Elementary," Mrs. Hull said smoothly.

Amanda admired her diplomacy. But it only served to make her want this child more. "Why?"

"Virginia sometimes exhibits inappropriate behavior."

Amanda looked past the teacher and principal to Virginia and stifled a laugh. Virginia was performing in the doorway for her classmates. She'd gathered her hair back and had puffed out her cheeks, rendering a startlingly accurate impersonation of Mrs. Hull.

Amanda cleared her throat. "She's not violent or anything, is she?"

"Of course not!" Virginia's teacher answered. "However—"

"However, I'm sure she'll do fine," Amanda said, raising her voice in warning.

Virginia caught her eye and whipped her arms down to her sides just as the other two women turned and walked back to her.

Amanda checked her watch. "Now, what time is school out?"

"Two thirty-five." The teacher looked as though it wouldn't be a moment too soon.

"All right, if we leave now, I can have her back—"

The principal was shaking her head. "You can't take this child anywhere now."

Amanda gripped the strap on her purse. "Now's a great time." She was careful to keep her voice even. "The lines for Santa won't be long. We might be able to visit two malls."

"Ms. Donnelly, I'm afraid you don't understand." The principal nodded a dismissal to Virginia and her teacher.

Amanda caught sight of Virginia's perplexed face as she returned to her seat. "You're right, I *don't* understand." *Calm down.* Amanda consciously lowered her voice and slowed her speech. "I thought we agreed that I could feature one of your students in my story. Naturally you or someone from the school will come along." Amanda made a mental note to tape footage of the principal. They could edit it out later.

"I'd like that, but today is out of the question."

"Why?"

Amanda spoke to the principal's back as the woman strode down the hall. *Great. Now you've alienated her and you'll have to start all over again at another school.*

Amanda lived in the fast pressured pace of the television studio and frequently forgot that the rest of the world didn't run on impossible deadlines.

She hurried after the principal, catching up just as the older woman entered her office. By the time Amanda reached the doorway, Mrs. Hull was behind her desk, pulling on a pair of glasses.

Amanda had clearly outstayed her welcome. Mentally shifting her schedule to allow for another school visit that afternoon, she started to thank the woman for her time.

Unbidden, a pair of blue eyes flashed in her mind, accompanied by a picture of the little blond scamp prancing in front of her classroom. *Virginia.* Too good to be true. Amanda knew she wouldn't be able to forget her. Furthermore, she'd probably spend days trying to find another child just like Virginia, fail, and end up back here in a week, anyway.

"Mrs. Hull, it's been a long time since I was in school, and I don't have children of my own. How can we get Virginia to the malls?" Amanda had deliberately said "we."

"*You* will need," Mrs. Hull said with the slightest bit of emphasis, "parental permission."

"Certainly." Amanda whipped out her notebook. "Do you have a telephone number?"

Mrs. Hull removed her glasses. "I don't have the school records in here, and even if I did, I wouldn't give you that information."

Deep breaths. Long deep breaths.

"And I'm concerned about Virginia's missing school," Mrs. Hull added.

So why hadn't she brought that up earlier? Amanda stopped breathing. Her brain was getting too much oxygen.

"Of course." Amanda managed a smile. "I'll discuss all that with her parents. I *am* permitted to speak to her parents?"

The principal favored her with a wintry smile, punched a button on the telephone and spoke. "Would you please look up the McEnerys' phone number and contact them for Ms. Donnelly?"

*McEnery.* Amanda wrote the name surreptitiously in her notebook.

"That's right," the principal was saying. "Well, call the father, then." She hung up the telephone. "The front office is just around the next corner," she informed Amanda in obvious dismissal.

Amanda gritted her teeth and smiled her way out. Passing gaily decorated bulletin boards, she located the front office.

A woman, bent over a file cabinet, straightened and removed a card. "Are you Ms. Donnelly?" she asked, catching sight of Amanda.

"Yes." Amanda, who had been tapping her pen impatiently, removed her hands from the counter.

The woman nodded and reached for the telephone.

*Hurry, hurry, hurry,* Amanda urged silently.

Kay had underestimated the amount of time necessary to produce this segment. Amanda looked at her watch again. It was obvious that she wouldn't be making any trip to a mall today.

On the other hand, it was still November, and the serious Christmas-shopping season had only begun. The timing on the Santa piece wasn't critical. Amanda just wanted to get this assignment over with. Malls were places to be avoided around Christmas.

Christmas had become overcommercialized and over-hyped, anyway. People expected too much of Christmas.

The school secretary waved to get Amanda's attention. "Mr. McEnery isn't in his office. Shall I leave your number?"

Amanda rattled off the studio number. "When is he expected back?"

"They don't know. He's showing houses today."

"He's a realtor?" Great. Erratic hours. They'd never connect.

"Apparently so," replied the secretary as she hung up the phone.

"Doesn't he have a cellular phone?"

"I didn't ask."

Amanda would have to count on the efficiency of his office staff. "What about Virginia's mother? Does she work outside the home, too?"

The school secretary checked the card. "She's deceased."

"Oh." Poor little kid. "Well, thank you for your time. If you'll tell me what agency Mr. McEnery's with, I'll contact him myself."

"I can't give out that information."

Amanda stared at the woman. "But you said he's a realtor. What if I wanted to buy a house from him?"

"School policy prohibits us from releasing personal information about our students," the secretary intoned.

"That's—"

Amanda's protest was interrupted when a teacher appeared in the connecting doorway. "The copy machine's out of paper."

"Did you look in the cabinet?"

The teacher nodded. "It's empty, too."

"I'll have to get more out of the supply room." The secretary grabbed a set of keys and jingled through the connecting door.

Amanda's gaze remained on the desk where the card containing the personal information of Virginia McEnery gleamed whitely.

No one was around.

Spying in an elementary school—how low had she sunk? Pretty low, she thought, ducking under the counter.

*McEnery Realtors,* she read on the card. That was all the information she needed. Good grief, she could look up the number in the telephone book herself.

Amanda virtuously avoided reading Virginia's home telephone number or address and stepped back to her side of the counter. "I'm on my way to the studio if anyone calls for me," she informed the returning secretary.

That was entirely too easy, Amanda thought, as she drove to the "Hello Houston" studio. For all their insistence on school security, Amanda already knew a lot about Virginia. She knew when school was out, how old the child was, that her mother was dead, who her father was, where he worked, the fact that he kept irregular office hours. And, if she'd wanted to, she could have learned their home address and telephone number. Come to think of it, no one had asked for Amanda's identification, either. She'd just waltzed into the school with a business card and nothing more.

*School Security. How safe are your children?* Now *that* was the kind of story she'd rather be doing. In fact...

By the time she pulled into the station parking lot, Amanda had thought of possibilities for an entire series of reports. When she reached her desk, she was surprised to find a message on her voice mail from Kirk McEnery.

That was quick. Obviously the man checked in with his office throughout the day. Amanda placed a return call.

He wasn't in. She left a message and went to work on another segment, set to air the next day.

When she discovered she'd missed his next call, she became impatient with their game of telephone tag and looked up the address of McEnery Realtors. They were located in the Memorial area—about half an hour from her Southwest Freeway studio. After leaving one more frustrating message, Amanda decided to drive there.

The traffic on the Houston freeways was already thickening. Amanda sighed, knowing the return drive in rush hour would be tedious.

This trip had better be worth it, she thought, parking her car in the lot of the small one-story building. Glancing at the other cars, Amanda noticed a few Mercedes, a BMW and a Lexus. Nice clientele, but then, Memorial was a nice area. Far out of her reach.

Slamming the door of her car—a modest import—she entered the tree-shaded building.

Ritzy place, she thought immediately. Calming blues and grays projected an air of elegance and no doubt soothed frazzled nerves. The dense carpet muted noise from telephones and computer printers.

"May I help you?" asked a woman who could have been standing behind the cosmetics counter at a department store.

Amanda felt windblown and a bit limp. "I'm Amanda Donnelly with 'Hello Houston.' Kirk McEnery, please."

"Mr. McEnery is out of the office with a client," the woman said smoothly. "Could I help you?"

Amanda shook her head. "We've missed each other all day. Will he be checking in soon?"

"Possibly." The woman regarded her with undisguised curiosity. After a moment, she gestured to a seating nook. "Would you like to wait?"

"Thank you." Amanda had planned to wait, anyway.

The mirror opposite the chairs confirmed her windblown appearance and the fact that she'd chewed off her lipstick. Tucking her chin-length hair behind her ears, she sank into a large plush chair and picked up the telephone on the lamp table. When she was put on hold, she closed her eyes, thinking that it would be easy to fall asleep in such a chair.

"Amanda!"

Amanda's eyes snapped open. "Yes, Kay?"

"*What* are you doing? You've spent hours trying to find a kid. There're a million kids in Houston. What's your problem?"

"Finding the right kid. I did. Now I'm getting permission from her father."

"Still?"

Amanda sighed.

"If it's that much trouble, go to the next kid on your list."

"The list is real short."

"So's lead time."

"Tell you what, Kay. Give this piece to somebody else. Maybe Maria Alvarez. I've got a great new idea I'd like to develop—"

"Oh, no. I specifically picked you for this assignment, Scroogette. You need some Christmas cheer."

"Cheer, shmeer. I'm saving it for Arbor Day. *That's* the time to decorate trees."

"Amanda—" Kay sighed her name "—what am I going to do with you?"

"Promote me to producer," Amanda suggested promptly. *I'm already doing producer work,* she thought but didn't say. They'd had this conversation before, and Kay was well aware of Amanda's ambition.

"Be patient. Maria's been with 'Hello Houston' longer than you. She's paid her dues."

And Maria was already a *senior* producer. Amanda made a face and shifted in the chair. She knew for a fact that she and Maria Alvarez were the same age. But Maria had started working at the station right after college. Amanda's career had been delayed a few years.

"I know," she said now. "Listen, I'll stop back by the station before I go home. This shouldn't take too long."

Amanda hung up the phone, hoping she spoke the truth. She refused to consider the possibility that Kirk McEnery would deny permission. What doting parent wouldn't be thrilled to have his child singled out for an appearance on television?

After a few minutes, Amanda began wiggling her toes in her shoes. She hated inactivity. She'd already wasted enough time in her life. There were other phone calls she could make, but there wasn't much privacy, even though the receptionist was diligently ignoring her.

Carefully fanned out on the low coffee table were real-estate magazines and wonderful new listings in the local housing market.

Amanda wasn't in the market for a house. Amanda was in the market for a small girl to rate Santa Clauses.

Her gaze darted around the open area, fastening on a wall full of plaques. Listing Leader of the Month, Listing Leader of the Year, Sales Leader, Million-Dollar Club and others. She searched for and found Kirk McEnery's name, engraved more than once. So, was he just a member of the family firm, or did he own it?

She found her answer almost immediately under a photograph of a baseball team in uniform. That plaque thanked sponsor Kirk McEnery, owner of McEnery Realtors. It also appeared that Kirk McEnery was a past president of the Houston Board of Realtors. Well, she'd already figured out that he was a busy man.

At five-thirty, there was a mass exodus from the building. The receptionist approached Amanda. "I'm going home. Would you like to leave a message or continue waiting? Some of the brokers will be here for a while yet.''

Amanda hesitated. She'd already invested half a day in this project and had nothing concrete to show for it. She hated to quit now. ''I'll wait,'' she said just as the door opened and a dark-haired man rushed in.

Equally dark eyes swept the entire reception area before a vaguely familiar voice demanded, ''Where's Virginia?''

# CHAPTER TWO

THIS COULD ONLY BE the elusive Kirk McEnery. Amanda caught herself searching the reception area for Virginia.

The receptionist looked startled. "She's not here. Was one of us supposed to pick her up today?"

"Someone *did* pick her up. I just don't know who." Completely ignoring Amanda, Virginia's father strode to the nearest desk and grabbed a telephone, jabbing at the buttons before even bringing the handset to his ear.

"This is Kirk McEnery. Virginia isn't at my office. I want to know who took her."

Fascinated by someone even more impatient than she was, Amanda watched the unfolding drama.

"I can't believe you didn't get a name," he snapped. "Give me a complete description."

He waited, his eyes squeezed shut, his jaw immobile. "What color hair did this woman have? Was she old? Young? What was she wearing?"

Amanda felt prickles of alarm. This was more than mere impatience. Had Virginia been kidnapped? It looked like the *How safe are your children?* story was long overdue.

"So you just *assumed* it was a woman? No one there saw who Virginia left with?" Kirk exploded in anger. "That's no way to run a day-care center!"

There was utter silence in the agency. The few people who remained stood unmoving in doorways, unapologetically eavesdropping.

Kirk paced as far as the telephone cord would allow. "I'm going to put you on hold and call my home. You'd better hope Virginia's there." He jabbed more buttons and shoved his hand into his pocket. "Eleanor? Kirk. Is Virginia with you?"

Kirk's body sagged and his sigh of relief was echoed by everyone there. "No, everything's fine. Don't hold dinner for me." He leaned against the desk and pressed another button. "Hello? She's at home. My housekeeper picked her up." Nodding, he rubbed his temple. "Yes, I'm aware that she's on the list of people approved to remove Virginia from the premises. No, I don't want Mrs. Webster's name taken off the list. Sure. Thanks."

Quietly replacing the telephone, Kirk rubbed his temple a moment more. People withdrew from the doorways. The receptionist looked as though she'd like to slip out unnoticed, but caught Amanda's eye.

"Kirk?" the woman began softly. "The 'Hello Houston' woman is here." She gestured toward Amanda.

"Hmm?" He swiveled toward the club chairs and noticed Amanda, apparently for the first time.

For a moment, Amanda saw the real Kirk McEnery, unguarded and still recovering from the tense seconds that had just passed. Relief mingled with the remnants of worry on his face, before his expression changed into a professional mask, and he slipped into his salesman persona.

"Ms. Donnelly?" He advanced toward her, hand outstretched. "Kirk McEnery."

"Amanda, please."

"Amanda." He took her hand in his, holding it just the correct amount of time, grasping it with just the correct pressure. It was a calculated handshake, assuring the other person that he was a strong, competent, but not overpowering man.

It was, in fact, identical to the handshake Amanda used. Perhaps Kirk realized it, because he hesitated briefly after breaking contact.

The funny thing was that several moments passed before Amanda realized they were no longer touching. Vibrancy hummed in the air around them. In Kirk, Amanda recognized a person who was driven to make things happen. On the outside, he might appear calm, but inside, thoughts flew. She detected the impatience he struggled to conceal.

Smiling, she realized he didn't do any better a job of hiding impatience than she did. She decided to dispense with time-wasting preliminaries. "I wanted to speak to you about a project involving your daughter, Virginia."

"My office is in the back." He guided her down the hall after waving off the receptionist. "I suppose you overheard the mix-up."

Amanda could hardly help but hear, and he must have known it. "One side, anyway. I imagine it's hard to be a single parent."

Kirk darted a sharp glance at her.

"The school told me," Amanda explained.

Opening the glass door to his office, Kirk stepped back to allow her to enter first. "The day-care center closes at six. It's difficult to get there by six, and if I'm showing houses, one of the gals here usually drives over and gets Virginia."

Amanda heard the "gals," but decided not to hold it against him.

He shrugged as he sat in a chair on the same side of the desk as she was. "Actually, I'd forgotten my house-keeper was picking her up this afternoon. Virginia had a dental appointment."

"When did you remember?"

Kirk gave her a rueful grin. "As soon as Mrs. Webster answered the phone."

Amanda couldn't help responding to the grin. "You covered well."

"This time," he responded, sitting back in the chair and regarding her.

His intense dark eyes reminded Amanda that the fea-ture that had initially drawn her to Virginia had been her *blue* eyes. Virginia must be the living image of her dead mother. Amanda glanced at the cabinet behind Kirk's desk to see if there were any family photographs. None. Just an astonishingly large bowl of candy-coated choco-lates.

His silence told Amanda that chitchat time was over. She studied him as she thought about the best way to voice her request. She guessed that he wasn't the type of parent who would be gushingly thrilled to have his child on television. He had no need to bask in reflected glory.

A raised eyebrow prompted her.

"'Hello Houston' is doing a feature rating the Santa Clauses in area malls. We decided to consult with the ex-perts—kids. I visited Cameron Elementary, and Virgin-ia's teachers recommended her."

"They *did?*"

She couldn't lie. "Well...I interviewed Virginia and they have no objections, if you'll grant permission."

The corner of his mouth hinted at a smile. "How long did you speak with Virginia?"

"A few minutes. Frankly, I don't want a child who'll be intimidated by the camera."

"According to her teachers, Virginia isn't intimidated by anything."

Amanda cleared her throat. "They mentioned their concerns."

"I'll bet they did." Kirk chuckled, his face relaxing into attractive lines. "Tell me what this Santa business entails and what Virginia's part in it would be."

"For our kids' segment, we thought we'd rate the local Santas. We'll want footage of Virginia talking with two or three of them. The rest she can visit off camera. We'd have to see how it goes." As she outlined her plans for the story, Amanda studied Kirk's face for his reaction. She liked to be flexible and was cautious about promising too much or being too specific, especially when children were involved.

She wasn't certain what Kirk's thoughts were, but got the impression that he would be an easy parent to work with. "The piece should air at the end of the week and might be repeated on the local news."

Kirk nodded. Amanda was right; he wasn't overly awed by the thought of his daughter being on television.

"The principal isn't eager for Virginia to miss school, so we'd have to spread the taping out over several afternoons. I think crowds will be smaller on a weekday than on a Saturday. Would that be a problem?"

He shrugged. "Not that I can see."

Amanda breathed easier. Considering how much trouble she'd already gone to, this part was easy. "Great. Let's start with Woodbrook Mall. It's the closest one to the studio. Is tomorrow all right?"

"It's fine with me if it's fine with Virginia."

*Virginia.* "Oh. We haven't told Virginia. We didn't want to disappoint her if we had to use someone else."

"I'll tell her this evening." He leaned forward. Amanda recognized it as her cue to hurry up. He was ready to move on to something else.

"Here's my card." She pulled one from the case she kept within easy reach. "Contact me if you have any questions. And if Virginia has a Christmas outfit, or just something red or green, could she wear that tomorrow?"

Kirk's face was blank. "I'll look in her closet," he offered cautiously.

"I'm sure you'll find something." Amanda stood and smiled. "I'll meet you at the west entrance to the mall around three o'clock."

"Hold it." Kirk was in the act of standing, too. "You'll *meet* me at the mall?"

"Yes. You're bringing Virginia."

Kirk inhaled deeply. "I assumed you'd drive her there."

Amanda was taken aback. She was a virtual stranger, and he was trusting her with his daughter. After all the protection—such as it was—the school had insisted upon, it seemed rather cavalier.

But that was it. He obviously assumed that she'd been checked out by the school. He'd be shocked to discover how wrong he was. She'd heard the concern in his voice when he was trying to locate his daughter. She'd *seen* a shaken father collect himself after hanging up the phone.

Amanda's heart beat faster as idea after idea popped into her mind. She'd propose that her story on child safety stretch at least a week. It was amazing how an innocuous piece like this Santa thing could lead to something truly big.

"I could drive Virginia to the mall if you like," Amanda managed to answer Kirk. "But I thought you'd want to be there."

"Hmm." He walked around to his desk to consult a large calendar.

Amanda took the opportunity to study him. His dark hair was businessman short and only a few silver threads glinted in the fluorescent light. He was good-looking, on the lean side, and would appear to advantage on camera.

And Amanda definitely intended to return and interview him for her child-safety report. *Working parents—who takes your place? Single parents—how do you cope?* She mentally rubbed her hands together in anticipation. Just as soon as she was finished with this Santa bit—

"I don't have anything formally scheduled after two o'clock tomorrow. However, I don't have unlimited time at my disposal. How long will this session take?" he asked, his voice crisp.

A vague "Not too long" response wouldn't do here. "That depends on the crowds, equipment set-up time and Virginia herself. I'll have to coach her, clip on her mike, and then we'll do a couple of takes from different angles." Amanda hesitated. Time was obviously a concern to him. "Realistically, you should allow at least two hours."

Kirk's brows drew together as he ran his finger down the blocks of time on his calendar. "And you want to do this at each mall?" he murmured.

"As I said, I doubt we'll tape Virginia with every Santa, but she'll have to visit them all."

"That's asking rather a lot, isn't it?"

Most parents would be thrilled, Amanda grumbled to herself. Trust her to find that one parent in a hundred who was unimpressed by the idea of his little darling on television.

"Why don't we see how tomorrow goes before we make more plans?" she offered, never doubting that he'd succumb to the lure of television like everyone else.

"All right then, Amanda, I'll see you tomorrow," Kirk said, reaching over his desk to shake her hand.

"West entrance, three o'clock," Amanda reiterated, thinking that she looked forward to it.

"I *KNOW* I TOLD HIM the west entrance at three." Amanda examined her watch again, her action mirrored by the lighting/audio technician and the cameraman.

"It's ten after. You think we should set up?" Ron, the cameraman, shifted the strap on his equipment.

Biting her lip, Amanda nodded. "Get some mall footage. We can use it for filler. Keep an eye out for a man and a little blond girl. Maybe they're waiting down at Santa's house."

Could she have missed them? Amanda scanned the parking lot, which was crowded, but by no means full. Traffic hadn't been that bad on the freeways.

She was torn between waiting by the entrance and going to a phone to call her office and check for a message.

Or call Kirk's office and leave a message.

She reached into the right pocket of her black pants, closing her fingers over a smooth oval stone with an indentation in its center. A worry stone. It was either that, or bite her fingernails, and Amanda was desperately trying to grow them. Maria Alvarez had perfect medium-length nails, which were always professionally manicured.

Amanda was aware that it was possible to have acrylic nails, but what would be the point until she conquered her nail-biting habit? She couldn't run off to a manicurist every day.

Searching the parking lot again, Amanda rubbed her thumb back and forth across the smooth stone. Her other pocket contained a similar stone, but her left hand held a clipboard, and that ought to keep her fingers out of her mouth.

*Where are they?* It was three-twenty and the stone in her pocket was warm from the constant rubbing.

She couldn't stand this inactivity.

Abruptly turning away from the west entrance, Amanda headed for the mall crossroads and the poinsettia mountain growing at the center. Benches circled the area under the skylights. Amanda positioned herself so she could stare at the mall entrance and monitor the Santa line on the north end at the same time.

Ron was already attracting attention, though he hadn't even set up all his equipment.

Christmas music resonated from the sound system. If she listened carefully, Amanda could hear the different music some of the individual stores piped in. The battle of the Christmas carols. Not to mention those stupid electric bells that clanged out a never-changing series of holiday songs played with the same twelve notes.

Amanda hated Christmas. Oh, not the real Christmas, the religious one, not even the commercialism of the holiday. Stores were just trying to make a buck. It was the frantic "biggerness" of it all. More lights, more decorations, more parties, more television specials, more giving, more getting.

More perfection. True perfection could never be attained because each year people expected more. And it was never enough.

Christmas was like a giant balloon that kept getting inflated. Eventually it had to pop.

It had popped for Amanda the year she was twenty-two—the final Christmas of her marriage.

Even now, nine Christmases later, the thought of it was enough to make her cover her face with her hands.

Stupid. Naive. Pigheaded. Young. *I'm old enough to make my own mistakes.* Amanda winced at the echo of her youthful declaration. At the mistakes—whoppers, all. And afterward her parents saying, "We're not going to say we told you so." And then they did.

She just hadn't listened. She'd been in love. No one had ever been in love like this before. Her husband even had a lovely name: Trenton Whitfield Barrington III. And she'd been Amanda Barrington, the name of a dowager something or other.

She lowered her hands from her face. Christmas hadn't gone away and neither had her memories.

It was hard to avoid them here at the mall. No matter where she looked, there was a jewelry store running a special on gold chains. How many gold chains did the world need, anyway?

Sighing, she checked the west entrance, the Santa house and her watch. Nothing had changed but the watch, which had advanced another twelve minutes, making Mr. McEnery and his daughter now thirty-three minutes late.

Her watch was very precise. It had been a gift from herself. A reminder of her wasted years.

Traffic had picked up in the mall. There was little aimless window-shopping. Most people strode from store to store with a sense of purpose, mentally reviewing their shopping lists. Or maybe searching for that one perfect present, just as she had done that long-ago Christmas.

Money had been tight during her brief, youthful marriage. Once the flowers had withered from the too-expensive wedding, once her college friends had returned to school and Amanda had moved into the small apartment with the rented furniture, reality had set in.

Marriage was nothing like the romantic dream she'd thought it would be. She'd moved clear across the country from her family and friends. Her file-clerk job barely paid for food and rent, and she soon learned the value of a dollar earned.

Her husband did not. Trenton Whitfield Barrington III was not used to practicing economy. Frankly, neither was Amanda, and their wedding money was quickly and foolishly spent.

After that, Trenton cut back on his course load and got a part-time job. After one semester of that, Amanda realized his schooling would stretch on for years. If he could carry extra classes, the struggle would be over sooner. Telling herself she was investing in their future, she took on an additional part-time job so Trenton could take more classes.

*Stupid,* Amanda thought now, and stood up from the bench. She'd been so very stupid.

Slowly, circling the poinsettia mountain, she gazed unseeingly at the shoppers. Houston hadn't had a cold snap yet this season, and the stores were forced to mark down winter clothes to encourage business. Displays featuring sweater-clad mannequins surrounded by fake snow sought to boost the Christmas spirit.

It'd been different the last Christmas of her marriage. The snow had been real. Everything else had been fake.

Amanda paced faster around the poinsettias. She hadn't spent this much time in a holiday-decked mall since that hideous time, and it was making her nervous. Usually the first glint of tinsel sent her into hiding with a big batch of catalogs.

She muttered under her breath. What could have happened to Virginia and her father? They were almost an hour late.

If she looked at her watch, she'd know precisely how late they were, but Amanda didn't want to look at her watch. She didn't want to be reminded of that Christmas.

Drat. They were fifty-three minutes late. Amanda took a wry pleasure in knowing, even though it triggered memories. But hadn't she been engaged in a melancholy pity party for herself most of the afternoon?

If only the memories weren't as precise as her watch. But she didn't even have to close her eyes to see the crumpled charge receipt she'd found in Trenton's pant's pocket as she prepared to do the laundry. The startling amount on the receipt was burned into her mind. She'd thought she'd found the receipt for her Christmas present.

Of course, they'd promised not to spend a lot on each other—they'd always promised that. But Amanda had thought this was Trenton's way of thanking her for the three years of working and scrimping that would end with his graduation in the spring.

She'd bought him a shirt. She couldn't give him just a shirt for Christmas—not when he'd bought her a beautiful watch.

Only the watch hadn't been for her.

But she refused to think of that betrayal here and now. With a last glance at the west entrance to the mall, Amanda strode toward Santa's house.

Ron sat on a wooden bench, guarding his camera. The lighting/audio tech leaned against a wall. Neither was pleased.

"It's already after four," Ron said. "You're into overtime in another hour."

And thus over budget before they started. Amanda began to fume. "Why don't you take some more background footage of Santa?"

Ron pointed to Santa's house. A sign had been planted next to the empty throne. It read, "Santa's busy feeding his reindeer. He'll be back at..." A clock face with hands indicating four-twenty completed the message.

"What?" Amanda looked at the line snaking through the giant candy canes. "How can he take a break during the busiest time of day?"

Ron shrugged. The tech looked bored.

"Wait here," Amanda instructed. "I'm going to call the McEnery agency."

She headed for the public telephones, thinking she should have called Kirk long ago. If she hadn't been so busy wallowing in self-pity, she would have. It wasn't like her to waste time.

"Mr. McEnery isn't in the office. May I leave a message?"

Amanda thought of several unsuitable but highly satisfying messages she could leave. "This is Amanda Donnelly. We had an appointment for three o'clock at Woodbrook Mall and he hasn't arrived."

"One moment."

The receptionist was probably checking Kirk's calendar. Amanda *had* said Woodbrook, hadn't she?

"Ms. Donnelly?" The receptionist's voice sounded in Amanda's ear. "He does have a note about meeting you.

However, I see that he was to show a house at two-thirty.''

Mentally reviewing yesterday's conversation with Kirk, Amanda thought she remembered him saying he was free after two o'clock. "Would you please tell him I called?"

Next she contacted her office. No message from Kirk.

The muted babble of the mall enveloped her after she hung up the telephone. Incessant holiday music assaulted her ears. Lights twinkled, decorations glittered, and Amanda steamed.

She'd actually been a little worried. Something might have happened to Kirk and Virginia on the way to the mall, but as soon as the receptionist said he'd planned to show a house at two-thirty, Amanda knew he was out with clients.

What she didn't know was if he'd forgotten or just ignored her.

And what about Virginia? Poor little kid. Waiting, just like Amanda was.

"Ho-ho-ho!"

Santa back from feeding the reindeer, no doubt. Her watch said four-twenty-five. Even he was late.

Amanda couldn't stand it anymore. "Ron?" She caught her cameraman's attention.

He raised his eyebrows.

"Let's go." She jerked her head toward the poinsettia mountain.

With each step she took, Amanda's anger grew.

*Men.* You could never depend on them.

Or rather, you could depend on them to be undependable.

They piled into the "Hello Houston" van and drove back to the studio in silence.

When she reached her desk, Amanda listened to her voice mail, then thumbed through the message slips, searching for one from Kirk. Nothing. She glared at the telephone before snatching it up and calling his agency one more time.

"Mr. McEnery did check in, Ms. Donnelly. He's had a very busy afternoon."

Amanda waited for further explanation. After cooling her heels at the mall for an hour and a half, she felt she was entitled, but the receptionist didn't elaborate.

The silence stretched as Amanda tried to compose a suitable message. Then, in the background on the other end of the telephone, she heard a familiar male voice, "I don't have time to deal with her now."

The receptionist instantly muffled the receiver, but Amanda was already openmouthed with indignation.

"Mr. McEnery is unavailable at the moment," the woman announced seconds later. "Would you care—"

A furious Amanda didn't listen to the rest. She grabbed her purse and car keys. So Kirk McEnery thought he didn't have time for her, did he?

# CHAPTER THREE

No APOLOGY? No message? No explanation?

Kirk McEnery's real-estate business must be doing *very* well if he could afford to alienate a member of the media.

And Amanda was extremely alienated.

She allowed herself to fume all the way out to the parking lot. Even snarled a bit as she gunned the engine of her car. But that was all. She needed to think, and rage clouded her thinking.

Besides, one should not drive on Houston freeways in a state of rage. Simply driving on Houston freeways was enough rage for anyone.

Diffusing her anger was much more difficult than she'd anticipated. She'd been stood up before, suffered disappointments before and worked on stories she didn't like before.

What was different about this one?

Why didn't she just pick another child and let Kirk explain to his daughter how his skewed priorities cost her the chance to be on TV?

Amanda was wasting her time. No wonder Kirk McEnery thought he could waste her time, too.

Standing her up was just . . . just . . . just such a typical *male* thing to do. And why should Virginia lose out on some fun because of her father's thoughtlessness? Besides, Amanda hadn't heard Kirk's explanation yet. Maybe it was a good one.

The stormy sky matched her mood as she arrived at McEnery Realtors. The winds of an incoming cool front blew brown pine needles across the asphalt parking lot. Amanda hoped it wouldn't rain. Nothing worse than lugging camera equipment around in the rain.

She pushed open the front door, already preparing to walk blithely past the receptionist.

Kirk and two couples stood near the waiting area. He was in the process of shaking hands with them.

Amanda stopped short. Were they coming or going?

Kirk's gaze flicked her way, then returned to the small group without giving Amanda a clue that he recognized her.

"May I help you?" the receptionist asked in dulcet, but pointed, tones.

Amanda stared at Kirk, but he still didn't acknowledge her. "I had a three-o'clock appointment with Kirk McEnery," she said, using a loud, clear voice to sound out each syllable of his name. She expected a reaction, but he didn't even flinch. "He's so conscientious that when he failed to arrive—or even send word—I was afraid he'd been in an accident."

There was silence as her words registered with everyone in the area. The receptionist looked toward the small group.

"I'm awfully relieved to see that he's all right," Amanda said, and beamed at Kirk.

He barely turned his head, but his eyes swiveled her way as he held her gaze without blinking.

Still staring at her, Kirk murmured something Amanda couldn't hear as the receptionist stood up from the desk. "Oh, dear," she cooed, as if she hadn't spoken to

Amanda already that afternoon. "Would you like a cup of coffee while we straighten out this mix-up?"

Amanda lost her staring contest with Kirk to respond to the receptionist. "No, thank you."

"Mr. McEnery will be with you in a moment, then."

And suddenly Amanda wasn't looking forward to the confrontation with Mr. McEnery.

She, who prided herself on professionalism under fire, had behaved unprofessionally. Furthermore, she'd probably blown her chances to tape Virginia, as well as to interview Kirk for the child-safety story.

After ushering the couples out the door, a decidedly cool Mr. McEnery approached Amanda. With a quick glance at his watch, he lifted an eyebrow at the receptionist. "Rosalie, could I impose...?"

"Certainly," Rosalie answered, grabbing her purse and scooting out the door.

Only after she left did Amanda realize how quiet the office was and how alone she and Kirk were.

She had come storming over here feeling she was owed an apology, and now she felt less than pleased with her behavior. Still, she'd been wronged. The best defense was a good offense and all that. She tilted her chin and fanned the embers of her anger.

Kirk regarded her unsmilingly, his eyes silently chastising her.

She hadn't remembered that they were so very dark. How could he have fathered a blue-eyed child? Surely, this man's genes would dominate.

"Our...appointment slipped my mind," he said at last. "I'm sorry." He didn't sound sorry.

She'd sat in the mall for all that time, and he wasn't even offering an explanation. Amanda felt she deserved an explanation. "We waited for an hour and a half," she pointed out. "I had a camera crew with me. An expensive camera crew."

"Your patience is commendable." And misplaced, she imagined him adding.

"I'm trying to do a story. I wish you'd called or left word for me here."

"Rosalie knew I was out with clients."

"Was I supposed to interpret that to mean you weren't coming or were just going to be late?"

"Naturally my clients come first. I assumed you'd realize that." He regarded her unsmilingly. "I apologize again for the misunderstanding."

"There was no misunderstanding! We were to meet at the mall at three o'clock. You didn't show up and cost me two hours of my time." More, if she factored in the preparation time.

His lips compressed. "And why are you here now? Are you in the market for a house?"

Amanda glared. The man was insufferable! "No." She was in the market for a good explanation and some penance on his part.

"I'm in the house-selling business." Indicating the front door, he said, "The couples who just left signed a contract this afternoon. The buyers wanted to see the house one more time."

Amanda knew she should drop the subject. But... "This was more than a casual trip to the mall with your daughter. She was counting on you." *I was counting on you.*

"The commission will be several thousand dollars," he disclosed. "While Virginia doesn't understand the importance of that now, she *will* benefit from the sale."

Amanda felt her lip curl. *Money.* He'd inconvenienced them and disappointed his daughter all for the sake of money.

Kirk's gaze caught her sneer. His eyes narrowed, and he crossed his arms over his chest. "Tell me, Ms. Donnelly. If you were on your way to film your Santa Claus story this afternoon and came upon, let's say, a wreck—a wreck with a tanker truck leaking chemicals—would you stop and investigate?"

She knew where he was going with this but answered honestly, anyway. "Yes."

"But Virginia and I are waiting at the mall. What about us?"

"I would have sent word," she protested.

"When?" he shot back.

"Sometime before an hour and a half had passed. *Or* when I radioed in the story, I would have left word with the studio receptionist to call you."

"At the mall?"

Amanda was silent. Getting a message to someone waiting at the mall would have been difficult, but not impossible. However, arguing was pointless. She'd accomplished nothing by coming here. She wanted groveling. But no matter what she said, he wasn't going to grovel because he wasn't the type.

She should leave. At once, while she still had an outside chance of making a graceful exit.

"That's all right," he said, holding both palms outward. "I understand how these unexpected events can crop up."

Listen to him! He was forgiving her, and she hadn't even apologized and didn't want to apologize. And she didn't like feeling as though she ought to, either.

"Seriously, my schedule is so erratic, I'd advise you to find another child to feature in your story." As he spoke, Kirk ushered her to the front door.

"Fine! I'll do just that," Amanda snapped. No, this hadn't gone at all well.

At that moment, the door opened, and Virginia and Rosalie entered.

"Daddy!" Virginia, dressed in a green sweat suit, a red bow in her hair, bounded over to him. "Is it time to go to the mall and see Santa?"

Kirk stared down at his daughter. Ah. How was Mr. I-had-more-important-things-to-do going to get out of this?

"I waited and waited. I thought we were going right after school. I gave Mrs. Hull my note, so I didn't get on the day-care bus. Was that okay, Daddy?"

"Uh, yes." The man who had verbally outmaneuvered Amanda was gone. In his place was one guilty-looking father.

"Mrs. Hull had to call Mrs. Rodriguez at day care. She was mad."

Amanda wondered who was mad and decided both women probably were. After all, she was. It appeared Kirk had a talent for making women mad.

After exchanging a look with Rosalie, who nodded to confirm Virginia's story, Kirk closed his eyes briefly.

"Are we going to go now? Huh?" Virginia slipped her hand into his and included Amanda in her question.

Over Virginia's head, a wary Kirk faced Amanda. She smiled serenely. *Bet you wish you'd groveled a bit now.*

"I can hardly wait!" Virginia gave a little hop. "I'm going to be on TV!"

*That's right, Virginia, back him into that corner.* Amanda's smugness vanished as a stricken expression crossed Kirk's features. She hardened her heart. *He* forgot. *He* stood her up. *He* didn't want to cooperate. *He* had told her to find another child. Let *him* explain, the cad. This ought to be good.

His lips parted. "Uh..." was all the eloquent Kirk McEnery could manage.

Virginia's hand touched Amanda's clenched fingers. Surprised, she automatically loosened them, and Virginia tucked her hand inside. "Let's go," she urged with a tug.

Amanda stared into those big blue eyes. The eyes of a motherless child. A motherless child who wanted to see Santa.

Amanda's heart softened. Of course, she'd known it would. She *was* human. "We can't go now," she said as gently as possible.

"Why not?" Virginia asked.

"Because." Amanda looked at Kirk, who, in typical male fashion, was being no help whatsoever. Coward. "Because... because Santa had an emergency."

"What kind of emergency?" Virginia wanted to know.

"One of his reindeer... stepped on an elf."

"Stepped on an elf?" Kirk repeated.

Amanda glared at him. She was trying to save his bacon. Couldn't he see that?

"Santa's got his *reindeer* at the mall?" Virginia's eyes widened.

"Well, not at the mall—"

"Then where are they?"

Good question. Too bad Amanda didn't have the answer.

"He had to take them back to the reindeer stables. It's time for them to eat," Kirk responded, surprising Amanda. "And it takes Santa a while to drive out there," he elaborated when Virginia seemed to accept this explanation.

Looking from one adult face to the other, Virginia asked, "Why can't one of the other elves feed the reindeer?"

It was Kirk's turn to blink. "Because..."

Virginia waited. Kirk's mouth worked.

"Because it's against union rules," Amanda said, coming to the rescue.

Rosalie, who'd been lingering by the door, began coughing. "I'm going home now," she said, ducking her head and yanking open the door.

Kirk had the strangest expression on his face. He ought to be grateful, the wretch.

"What's the union?" Virginia asked.

"It's a group of workers," her father answered.

"You mean Santa's workers? The elves?"

"Yes," Amanda said. "And the elves have a very powerful union. You don't mess with elves." She looked Virginia directly in the eye.

Virginia turned to her father.

"Ms. Donnelly's right. I make it a point never to argue with elves. They have nasty tempers," he added with unnecessary embellishment.

"They do?"

"Yes. And they're already mad about this reindeer thing," Amanda said, hoping Kirk would quit while they were ahead.

"Oh." Virginia mulled that over while Amanda and Kirk exchanged looks.

Amanda didn't have the slightest idea if Virginia believed them or was just humoring them. She still clung to their hands, preventing Amanda from making a getaway.

"Besides, the reindeer have to eat now and so do you."
Kirk dropped Virginia's hand and switched off the lights.

"Then when am I going to be on TV?" Virginia asked,
still holding Amanda's hand.

Amanda arched an eyebrow at Kirk.

He hesitated, his hand on the doorknob. "Tomorrow? Three o'clock?" His look dared Amanda to dis-
agree.

And of course she wouldn't. "West entrance. Woodbrook Mall." Kirk didn't deserve to get off so lightly.

But the smile he gave her was almost worth it.

"AMANDA DONNELLY, please."

"Speaking." Amanda wasn't the least surprised to hear
Kirk's voice on the other end of the line. She'd half expected him to call sometime this morning to thank her for
graciously saving his handsome hide yesterday. Until he'd
smiled, she hadn't fully appreciated how handsome that
hide was.

Propping her feet on her desk, Amanda sat back and
prepared to receive her accolades.

"M ... Amanda?"

"Hello, Kirk," she said cheerfully. He obviously
wondered if he could still call her Amanda, rather than
reverting to the Ms. Donnelly she'd been in their last
conversation. She'd encourage the informality. It might
make him feel guiltier.

"Amanda," he repeated, firmly this time.

She waited, a smile on her lips.

"I have a conflict this afternoon."

These weren't the words she wanted to hear.

"And I won't be available to drive Virginia to the mall
at three o'clock."

Amanda reached for a pencil, nearly snapping it. "Do we need to reschedule?" Honestly, this Santa story was entirely too much trouble.

Kirk drew a long breath. "I'd rather not. My schedule is so erratic—"

"How fortunate for you," Amanda said, knowing she shouldn't have.

There was a brief silence. "I've been trying to sell a rather unusual house in Memorial for more than two years," Kirk explained in a tone that said he didn't feel he owed her an explanation. "I have a potential buyer who wants to see it immediately after lunch."

"Congratulations."

He ignored her sarcasm. "If *you* can drive Virginia to the mall, I'll send a note to the school so you'll be allowed to pick her up."

"Then what?"

"I'll try to get there, but if I don't make it to Woodbrook by the time you're ready to leave, bring her back to the agency."

"Oh, goody. I've always wanted to run a taxi service on the side." Let him dispatch somebody from his office.

"You can always choose another child," he pointed out with maddening serenity.

Right, so he could blame *her* for Virginia's inevitable disappointment. Not this time. "Tell the school I'll be there."

After she'd hung up, Amanda sat a few moments longer, wondering how she, a reasonably intelligent woman, had been so neatly manipulated by one completely unreasonable man.

But however exasperated she might be with Virginia's father, Amanda shouldn't be angry with Virginia. She concentrated on tamping down her impatience as she drove to Cameron Elementary. The "Hello Houston" crew was headed for the mall with instructions to find Santa and sit on him, if necessary.

Turning the corner to the school, Amanda slammed on her brakes. A line of cars crawled through the circle drive. By the time Amanda realized that she was in line, she was trapped.

It was like an obstacle course, with mothers—Amanda noted the great number of women clad in business suits—dragging children between cars, vans and other children. Crossing guards beeped whistles and school buses lumbered past.

How could she get out of here? She couldn't. So she found herself inching along, glad it wasn't summer when her car would be in danger of overheating.

No wonder Kirk wanted to avoid this mess. Amanda fumed silently, annoyed that she seemed to spend an awful lot of mental energy being angry with Kirk McEnery.

At last she pulled in front of the school. A row of children sat on the concrete walk, backpacks beside them. Amanda spotted Virginia, wearing a non-Christmas outfit, but with the same holiday bow in her hair. Mentally positioning her on Santa's lap, Amanda decided that with the jolly old elf's arm draped around the little girl, no one would be able to see what she was wearing, anyway.

A car horn honked behind her. Mrs. Hull, the principal, approached Amanda's car. Virginia stayed where she was. Great. Did Kirk forget to take care of the red tape?

Mrs. Hull peered in the car. "Oh." She beckoned to Virginia. "Now don't forget to tell Santa that you go to school at Cameron Elementary," Mrs. Hull said as she checked to see that Virginia's seat belt was fastened.

"I won't," Virginia promised.

Mrs. Hull looked satisfied as she waved them off. Virginia settled into Amanda's car as if she'd done so many times before.

Amanda hardly knew how to handle such trust. "Hi, Virginia. Your dad couldn't be here, so he asked me to come and get you."

"I know." The blue eyes regarded her without surprise, question or concern.

It hit Amanda suddenly that these same circumstances must have occurred over and over again. She remembered snippets of conversation she'd overheard in the real-estate agency. A list of approved people...a housekeeper...Rosalie picking up Virginia when Kirk hadn't even voiced his request.

Amanda didn't know what to think. But it wasn't her business. Her business was taping this story. "Do you know why you're going to visit Santa?" Amanda asked.

"Because it's Christmastime," Virginia answered, making Amanda wonder exactly *what* she'd been told.

"Yes. A lot of boys and girls visit Santa at Christmastime. And—" Amanda stopped. She'd been about to blow the Santa myth sky high. Did Virginia still believe? Completely? How was Amanda going to explain all those Santas at all those malls?

"You know Santa has lots of helpers, don't you?" Amanda gingerly picked her way through the Santa-myth mine field.

"Yes." Virginia nodded. "The union."

Amanda bit her lip. "Right, the worker elves and all that. I was thinking more of the 'helpers.' He, uh, can't be everywhere at once."

They'd come to a stoplight, and Amanda glanced sideways to see how Virginia took this revelation.

"Oh, I know." Virginia shifted in her seat. "He's too busy right now making all the toys. That's why he sends his helpers to the mall."

"What do you think of those helpers?"

Virginia lifted a shoulder.

Hmm. Amanda merged onto the Southwest Freeway. "Do you think they do a good job?"

Virginia blew out her breath. "Sometimes." She shifted again. "I thought we were going to see the *real* Santa."

"The North Pole is a long way away."

"The North Pole! Give me a break!"

Amanda clutched the steering wheel, afraid to ask what Virginia meant. She was only six, right? She didn't sound six. She sounded thirteen. "Where do you think Santa lives?"

"Well, he lives there, but he checks out the malls to get the reports from his helpers."

"Reports?"

"On what kids want. Then he goes to the toy stores and tells them what to order."

Amanda decided not to comment on the twisted logic of commercially supplied toys versus Santa-supplied toys. "So the malls are just like big information centers."

"Uh-huh." Virginia nodded vigorously. "And sometimes he takes his helpers' place for a while."

Amanda thought she was beginning to understand the reasoning of a child. Facts with a fantasy twist. "Maybe to show them how to act like Santa Claus."

"Maybe."

Amanda eased into her request as she exited the freeway. "Well, Virginia, what we want you to do is find the best Santa's helper in Houston. Or even uncover Santa himself." She glanced down at the little girl, whose eyes were wide. "We need to talk about what makes a good Santa."

"His beard," Virginia said without hesitation. "Santa has a real beard."

"Okay," Amanda said, encouraging her. Spotting the "Hello Houston" van in the mall lot, Amanda found a place to park not too far away. "What else?"

"Well...his clothes. Once I saw a Santa in tennis shoes. The *real* Santa wears boots. And he should have a soft lap. He's fat, you know."

"Probably all those Christmas cookies he eats," Amanda murmured, thinking her own lap was getting a bit soft. "So, you'll be checking out his beard, his lap and his boots?"

"He should sound like Santa, too," Virginia said as they got out of the car. "And it's nice if he gives you a present after you visit with him."

"I'll guess you'll have to wait until Christmas morning for that."

"No, I mean, like a coloring book or stickers. Sometimes a candy cane."

"What's your favorite?" Amanda smiled down at the little girl.

Virginia responded by casually taking Amanda's hand. "A candy cane," Virginia said and grinned, revealing her missing tooth. It didn't look bad at all.

"A woman after my own heart. See if you can nab an extra one for me."

"Okay," Virginia said.

Once they reached the mall crossroads, Virginia looked both ways and headed unerringly for Santa's house.

Velvet ropes held in place by giant candy canes marked the path to Santa. He sat on a high-backed chair in front of a cottage that looked like the gingerbread house in an amateur production of *Hansel and Gretel*. Off to the side, Rudolph and a friend stared unblinkingly at the waiting children. Well, maybe the reindeers' eyes didn't blink, but Rudolph's nose did.

Virginia approached this scene warily. Amanda's cameraman, Ron, was already in place. He hoisted the camera to his shoulder, but at a signal from Amanda, the lights remained off. She didn't want to spook Virginia before preparing the little girl.

But Virginia appeared oblivious to the camera equipment. She picked up a handful of rubber snow and scratched the plastic foam of the candy canes. "Fake," she announced.

Amanda sighed.

"Where do we go next?" Virginia brushed the snow from her fingers.

"Whoa, we're not finished here. You haven't seen Santa yet."

"Don't need to. He'll be fake, too."

Oh, no. Waving at Ron to sit down, Amanda drew Virginia away from the scene. "Of course the props are fake!" she said in a hearty voice. "Real snow would melt and make a mess all over the floor and the candy canes would draw bugs."

"Can I go to the toy store?" Virginia had dismissed the Santa scene altogether and was pointing to a conveniently located purveyor of children's material dreams.

"No." Amanda sat on a circular bench surrounding a tree and pulled Virginia down next to her. Virginia ran her hands over the bark. "This is real."

Amanda captured her hands. The little girl reluctantly faced her. "Remember what we talked about? That you're looking for the best Santa in the malls? When you talk with him, listen to his voice, check out his boots and beard. Can you think of anything else to look for?''

Virginia shook her head.

''So you have a pretty good idea of the real Santa?''

''Oh, yes.''

Virginia spoke so confidently that Amanda was surprised. ''How?''

Virginia swung her legs. ''I'll just know.''

Amanda wanted something more concrete, but they'd feel their way this first time. ''Okay, then, let's talk about what will happen. You'll stand in line—'' but not for long, she thought, if Amanda had her way ''—and Ron over there... Do you see Ron?'' Amanda pointed and waved.

Virginia peered down the mall as the cameraman waggled his fingers.

''Yes, that's Ron. He'll take your picture when Santa is talking to you. Now, he has a very big camera, and it needs lots of light. There isn't enough light here in the mall, so we brought our own.''

Amanda pointed to the lighting tech, but the woman was staring into the window display next door. ''See the lights? Don't be startled when they come on. They're very bright.''

Virginia nodded.

Amanda stood and started walking back toward Santa. ''We want to hear you when you talk with Santa, so I'll clip a microphone to the strap of your jumper.''

''What do I say?''

''Just what you say when your dad takes you to see Santa.''

''He doesn't take me to see Santa.''

Amanda froze. ''It's still early,'' she said carefully. ''December doesn't begin until this weekend.''

"He's busy."

Swallowing rising anger, Amanda reminded herself that Virginia's situation wasn't any of her business.

"Grandma took me last year. And there was real snow."

An intriguing bit of information. Amanda wanted to question Virginia, but it was best not to comment on Kirk's parenting or pump Virginia for information on her family situation. And why should she be interested, anyway?

"We don't get snow much in Houston, do we?" As Virginia spoke, Amanda scanned the area and saw Virginia doing the same thing. *She's looking for her father.* Amanda knew, because she was looking for him, too.

And he was nowhere in sight.

# CHAPTER FOUR

HIS ABSENCE WAS no surprise, but Amanda didn't like to see Virginia disappointed. Apparently Kirk had no such qualms.

"Virginia, let's put you over here." Amanda positioned Virginia with Santa's gingerbread house in the background. "Stay there a minute."

Stepping away, Amanda turned to her cameraman. "Ron, tape some filler and let's see how she reacts to the camera."

With a nod, he positioned the camera on his shoulder. Amanda signaled for lights, expecting Virginia to squint or flinch.

But Virginia ignored everything in her search of the crowd.

Amanda hoped Kirk would come, but knew better. He had no intention of cutting his house-showing short. Fuming inwardly, she attached the microphone to the strap of Virginia's jumper. "Can you drop the cord inside?" Amanda asked. "Right beneath your arm."

Virginia threaded the microphone cord until it dropped past her knees. "Virginia—" Amanda bent to clip a plug to the cord "—when I spoke with your father, he didn't think he'd come until we were through. And he might not be here then, either." She straightened and stared down at the silent little girl. "But don't worry, if that happens, I'll take you to his office."

"Can't we wait a little longer?"

It was hard to deny the pleading in those big blue eyes, but Amanda had to. "We need to get started." She patted Virginia on the shoulder. "You'll do fine. Okay?"

Looking deflated, Virginia nodded.

Great. Amanda needed enthusiasm. Happiness. Muttering under her breath, she approached Ron. "How's she look?"

"Pale."

Amanda peered over his shoulder into the viewfinder. Blondes did wash out under the lights. "I've got some blusher in my purse." She set her notebook on the floor and dug in her shoulder bag.

"Is that makeup?" Virginia asked with renewed interest.

Amanda started dabbing pink on her cheeks. "Yup." Maybe this would distract her.

"I get to wear makeup?"

Amanda surveyed her handiwork. "Just for television."

"How do I look?" Virginia held her head at an angle and made kissing noises with her lips.

"Gorgeous." Amanda grinned and propelled Virginia toward the line of waiting children and their parents. A small sign announced that there would be a twenty-minute wait from the end of the line. Remembering Santa's reindeer-feeding break the day before, Amanda picked a spot in the line about five children away from Santa and positioned Virginia there.

"Hey!" The protests began immediately.

Amanda stuck out her hand toward the nearest mother and said the magic words. "Hi, I'm Amanda Donnelly with 'Hello Houston.' Could we tape your child as—" Amanda glanced down "—he waits in line for Santa?"

As she expected, the parents around them were more than cooperative. The parents out of camera range still grumbled.

Ron obligingly panned the waiting people. Amanda knew they'd edit later.

A green-clad elf carrying a camera wandered over. "Will you want her picture taken with Santa?"

"I think we've got that covered," Amanda answered, gesturing at her production crew.

The elf pressed closer to Virginia. "What are y'all doing?" She smiled at Amanda, Virginia, and especially the camera.

"Taping." Pointing to an impatient mother juggling two toddlers and a package-laden stroller, Amanda added, "I think you have a customer."

One eye on the camera, the elf waggled her fingers and reluctantly moved away.

Obviously influenced by the elf, Virginia struck poses for Ron. She acted thrilled to discover fake icing on the gingerbread house, peered into the windows and laughed uproariously at the mechanical toy makers. Amanda let her get it out of her system off camera.

Just before Virginia's turn with Santa came, Amanda whispered in her ear, "Remember, don't tell Santa what we're doing." As if Santa hadn't noticed a full production crew aiming a camera at him. But at least he wouldn't know he was being rated.

"Okay," Virginia whispered back, giving Amanda a thumbs-up.

Lights. Camera. "Hi, Santa!" Virginia shouted, blasting the sound meter.

The technician, wearing headphones, frantically signaled. Amanda caught Virginia's attention and brought a finger to her lips.

"Ho-ho-ho, little lady." Santa made a good effort, but his voice was no match for Virginia's. "Who're your friends?" Santa smiled at the camera.

Behind the display, a group of preteens jumped up and down, waving their hands. Wonderful. Everybody wanted to break into show business.

"Aren't you going to ask me what I want for Christmas?" Virginia tugged on Santa's beard. It slipped.

"Sure," Santa replied and negligently readjusted his beard, then settled Virginia on his lap.

She fingered the fuzzy lapel of his red suit, which looked grimy and cheap under the harsh glare of the lights. Next, she leaned over and looked toward the floor.

Amanda followed her gaze. Santa wore brown hiking boots.

"So, little girl, what can Santa bring you for Christmas?"

Virginia eyed him doubtfully. Amanda didn't blame her. Santa spent more time beaming at the camera than paying attention to the child on his lap.

This wasn't going to work. "Just a moment." Amanda stepped from behind the camera. "Santa, pretend we're not here. It's just you and *Virginia*." Amanda emphasized her name.

"Oh, Virginia, is it? A pretty name for a pretty girl." He bounced her on his knee.

"Hey!" Virginia grabbed the first thing she could. It happened to be his beard. Once again, it came loose.

Santa patted it back into place. "So, Ginny, what do you want to find under your Christmas tree?"

Virginia glared at him, her lower lip stuck out in a pout. "My name is Virginia, and I want a Super Nintendo."

"Ho-ho-ho. Wouldn't you like Santa to bring you a pretty doll? Though Santa will have to look hard to find a doll as pretty as you."

What a line. Amanda covered her mouth with her hand. *Santa and Sexism: A special holiday report.* Alliteration always went over with viewers.

Virginia wasn't smiling. No wonder. If all the Santas were as bad as this one, Amanda would hire her own. In fact, that might not be such a bad idea.

"I don't want a doll!" Virginia pushed at the velvet chest and tried to hop down. The green elf rushed to help Santa.

"Don't you want to stay and talk with Santa?" The elf warbled, smirking at the camera.

"No! He stinks!"

"Cut." Amanda ran to intervene. "Thanks very much," she said, firmly grasping Virginia's hand.

With a jerk of her head, Amanda signaled her crew to follow as she led Virginia away.

"That wasn't Santa," Virginia announced.

"I agree." Amanda stopped and unhooked Virginia's microphone.

"His beard was fake. His voice was fake. His shoes were wrong and he smelled bad."

"Probably hanging around the reindeer too much," Amanda murmured. "What do you think?" she asked Ron.

Never very vocal, he simply shrugged. The lighting/audio tech shook her head. They confirmed what Amanda suspected—they'd captured no more than a few seconds of usable material.

There wasn't enough time to visit another mall today. Studying the microphone plug in her hand, Amanda came to a decision. "Virginia, we're going to interview you. Ron, find a backdrop, and I'll hook her up again."

"What do you mean?" Virginia asked.

"I'm going to ask you questions about Santa and how that guy compares."

"I just *told* you. He st—"

"He stinks, I know. Tell us how he compares to the real Santa. I don't think you need to mention the fact that he smells."

"But he *does!*" Virginia's voice got louder. "I thought I was going to gag!" Amanda glanced around and found that the people at the end of the line were watching with rapt attention.

"Amanda."

She heard a soft whistle and saw her cameraman beckoning. He was standing by the display windows of a Christmas-decoration store.

Perfect.

They positioned Virginia in front of a white tree with silver ornaments and brought the camera down to her eye level.

"Pretend you're talking to your friends," Amanda instructed. "And look at me, not at the camera. Ready?"

At Virginia's nod, Amanda indicated that Ron should begin taping. "Virginia, tell the boys and girls listening what you expect when you visit Santa Claus."

"Well . . ."

*Please be bright and articulate,* Amanda pleaded silently, though she knew that was asking a lot of a six-year-old.

Then a miracle happened. Whether it was the small crowd of curious shoppers gathering to watch or Virginia blossoming with all the attention, she stood straighter and smiled confidently at Amanda. Then she launched into the qualities they'd discussed in the car earlier. Amanda couldn't have asked for more if she'd written a script.

"First of all, Santa should be fat, so his lap will be soft. He has a white beard and crinkly eyes. And he should smell like *peppermint*. When he says, 'Ho-ho-ho,' his voice should rumble. Santa wears black boots and his outfit should look nice for meeting us."

"What else?"

"Well, he should be interested in what you want for Christmas and...and he doesn't make promises he can't keep," Virginia finished obliquely.

"And how was the Woodbrook Santa?" Amanda asked.

"Oh, Amanda, puh-leez." Virginia rolled her eyes.

Amanda was startled to hear Virginia use her name, but decided it was cute and showed how relaxed she'd become in front of the camera.

"This guy must have flunked out of Santa school."

Amanda's jaw dropped. Virginia had become a little *too* relaxed.

Virginia adopted the confiding manner of a successful gossip columnist and ticked off the Woodbrook Santa's shortcomings.

Cute, smart-alecky kids. A lethal combination. Amanda had no idea how much usable footage she'd get.

After a few more questions—though Virginia didn't need prompting—Amanda called it a day. "I'm going to check in at the studio before we leave here," she said, heading for the pay phones.

She left Virginia with Ron while he put away his equipment. Amanda planned to call the studio, yes, but she also wanted to check to see if Kirk had managed to make it to the mall.

He hadn't, apparently.

She stood at the mall crossroads, staring from the never-ending line for Santa—now on his reindeer-feeding break—to the west entrance of the mall. With a sigh, she headed for the public telephones.

Catching sight of her watch as she punched in the "Hello Houston" number, Amanda closed her eyes and leaned against the gray-tiled wall. Great. It'd be five o'clock by the time they left. She didn't look forward to the drive on traffic-clogged freeways.

"No messages from Kirk McEnery?" she asked the receptionist after hearing the names of people who'd phoned and noting that Kirk wasn't among them.

"No," the receptionist answered. "But Kay said for you to get over here as soon as you finished."

What did her executive producer want now? Amanda wondered, running her fingers through her bangs. It would take at least an hour to drop Virginia off at her father's office and return to the studio. "Did Kay mention what she wanted?"

"No, but she did say to tell you to haul your—"

"I get the picture."

Ron and Virginia weren't where she'd left them. The tech, left guarding the equipment, pointed. "He took her to get something to drink."

Amanda felt guilty as she walked toward the food court and spotted Ron and Virginia at a small atrium table. The little girl had been very cooperative, and Amanda hadn't even thanked her.

Virginia drank a frozen berry slush from a cup about as big as she was. Ron had a soft drink.

"Hi," Amanda said, sliding onto the third stool.

Virginia raised her eyebrows and kept sucking on her straw.

Watching her, Amanda came to a decision. "Virginia, how'd you like to visit a TV studio?" The little girl could have a treat, and Amanda could find out what Kay wanted.

"You mean where they make TV shows?"

Amanda nodded. "Just like the one you'll be on."

"Sure!"

Virginia babbled during the entire drive to the studio. Thank goodness it was a short drive. They parked in Amanda's usual spot, and Virginia ran on ahead to the door and waited, hopping from one foot to the other.

Virginia's enthusiasm as they passed the security guard reminded Amanda of her first day on the job. She hadn't been an associate producer then. No, she'd been a receptionist and gofer.

But that was fine. It'd meant she had a foot in the door, and that was her goal. Then.

She'd gone back to school after her divorce, continuing her degree in radio/TV/film. Thinking it would help to have work experience in television when she applied for a job after graduation, she offered to take any position. Without pay.

In six weeks, she was on the payroll.

There was so much time to make up. So many courses to take. Juggling work and school had been hard, but easier than juggling two jobs and a marriage.

The long hours helped her to forget her failed marriage and kept her out of her empty apartment. Observing the popular Maria Alvarez had helped Amanda set her goals.

Kay had been so impressed with Amanda's enthusiasm that she'd promised her a job in production after graduation. That had been six years ago.

"Virginia," she called when the little girl galloped too far ahead. "Here's my office."

Virginia turned back and followed Amanda into a spartan cubicle. "That's it?"

"I don't need much," Amanda said, wiping the image of Maria's big corner office from her mind.

"This is where they make TV shows?"

"No." Amanda flipped through her messages and assorted papers on her desk. "You saw those big tall black doors on the other end of the hall?"

"Uh-huh."

"Those are the studios. I'll show you one in a minute."

"I want to see it now!"

"In a minute." Amanda reached for the telephone. "I want to check with my producer, then call your dad." She pointed. "Scrape off that chair and have a seat."

Looking disappointed, Virginia crept over to the chair and stacked the assorted files and papers onto the floor.

Amanda felt a pang of guilt at the little girl's expression. It was such a picture of stoic disillusionment that Amanda wondered how many times Kirk had done the same thing.

Just then, Kay answered her telephone.

"It's Amanda. What's up?"

As Amanda listened to the latest crisis, Virginia stood and edged toward the door. Putting her hand on the knob, she looked at Amanda.

Shaking her head, Amanda held up a finger, then was distracted by Kay's question.

"Just a sec. I've got that info around here somewhere...." Amanda turned to dig in the piles of papers behind her, then stretched the telephone cord over to the pile Virginia had made by the chair. Kneeling and cradling the phone between her shoulder and her ear, Amanda searched through the papers, withdrawing a file in triumph.

"Yes, they listed two contacts."

"Great. We can't reach the primary contact, and I don't want to be left with three minutes of dead air."

"Okay, I'll call number two," Amanda offered.

As she scribbled Kay's instructions, Amanda was aware that Virginia had slipped out the door.

That was all right. The little girl's bright head was visible just above the lower edge of the rectangular window in Amanda's door.

"Coming, Virginia," she called, still scribbling. "Let me phone your dad and I'll be right with you."

As Kirk's agency number rang, Amanda perched on the corner of her desk. What a day. And it wasn't over yet.

"Kirk McEnery."

Amanda was startled not to hear the receptionist's voice.

"Amanda Donnelly. We finished at the mall and I brought Virginia back to the studio with me." Amanda glanced through the window. Virginia had wandered a few feet away, but was still visible.

"I thought you were going to bring her here." Annoyance sounded in his clipped tones.

*And I expected you to come to the mall.* Reviewing their previous conversation, Amanda said, "I don't believe we actually settled that. I can bring her to you there, but I won't be able to leave for a while."

"How long is a while?"

"An hour." Actually, Amanda thought she'd finish long before then, but let Kirk wait on *her* for a change.

Silence, then, "I'll drive over there." *And I'm not happy about it,* his tone implied.

Amanda didn't care.

"Virginia will be hungry."

Well, Amanda did care about that. "She hasn't complained. She had a giant slush drink at the mall."

"How nutritious."

"There was fruit in it." *Don't tell me you've never fed her junk food.* What a hypocrite. Amanda would bet that Virginia had waited longer and later on her father than she'd wait this evening.

Her phone buzzed. "That's my producer. I'll have to take this call." He wasn't the only one who was busy.

"By all means." His voice stopped just short of sarcasm. "See you in a bit."

Amanda broke the connection. Kay's questions only took seconds, but when Amanda opened her door, Virginia was nowhere in sight.

Which way did she go? "Virginia?" Amanda couldn't raise her voice, not in a television studio.

No answer.

She gazed toward the main entrance of the building, then chose to walk in the other direction. "Virginia?" Amanda stopped to listen and heard nothing. "I can take you on your tour now."

Still nothing. Amanda pursed her lips in annoyance. "It's not a good idea to play hide-and-seek here. There are too many cords. You could get hurt."

She'd entered the black cavernous area behind the individual studios. The ceiling soared several stories above her. Thick cables looped over girders like vines in the jungle. Blackout curtain lined the walls. There were a million places to hide.

Where was Virginia?

Several of the studios had red lights illuminated above the three-story tall doors. Filming was in progress.

Amanda groaned. If Virginia had opened one of the doors, she'd spoil whatever was going on inside. As it was, Amanda couldn't open them without knowing for certain whether Virginia was inside.

"Virginia!" Amanda swatted at curtains and peered behind prop boxes for countless minutes, trying to convince herself that Virginia was playing a game. Any moment, she'd jump out and scare the bejeebers out of Amanda.

This was taking too long. It was time to try bribery. "Virginia, if you can hear me...you win. How about coming out and I'll treat you to..." What did little girls like to eat? Amanda tried to remember and couldn't. "Pizza."

No response. Well, pizza sounded like a good idea whether or not Virginia emerged from her hiding place. "Remember, it takes about half an hour for it to be delivered. The sooner you come out, the sooner I can call in the order." She slowly turned in a complete circle, searching for a telltale flutter of curtains or the tapping of small, six-year-old feet. "I'm not calling the pizza place until you come out."

She crossed her arms and stood among all the wooden crates and backdrops.

No Virginia.

That did it. The Santa piece had just become a one-shot thirty-second blurb about the Christmas season and all the kids who like to visit Santa. Kay probably wouldn't run it, but Amanda didn't care. This experience had only reinforced her opinion that children were highly overrated.

Okay. Okay, now she was getting desperate. "Virginia, you were great today. So great that *I'll* buy you a Super Nintendo. How about it? When we finish the last Santa visit, we'll go pick one up." How much did they cost, anyway?

Amanda rolled her eyes. At this point, cost wasn't an issue.

When Virginia didn't leap at her shrieking in delight, Amanda knew she wasn't in the area. Lightly running the length of studio row, Amanda reached the intersection of another hallway. It was time for the six-o'clock news. If Virginia somehow messed *that* up...

Amanda didn't want to think about the consequences. Looking right, then left, she tried to figure out which direction would appeal to a six-year-old. On the other hand, maybe Virginia had gone back to the guard at the front entrance.

That was it. Sure. She'd felt lonely and had sought someone to talk with.

Snatching at an in-house telephone, Amanda buzzed the guard. "Have you got a little blond girl up there with you, Hank?"

"No, ma'am, but I do have an angry fella here."

Kirk. Amanda winced.

"Been callin' your office. Someone's got to escort him. I got no one to relieve me."

"I'm on my way."

This was the cherry on the cake of her day. Dodging electrical cables, Amanda ran to the guard station.

A thin-lipped Kirk awaited her. His gaze flicked around her. "Virginia?"

"Uh..." Amanda tucked her hair behind her ear. "She wanted to see the studio."

"Is she about finished?"

"No." Amanda swallowed.

Kirk pointedly held up his watch. "It's getting late. Perhaps she could complete her tour another time?"

"Oh, but—"

"Where is she?"

Amanda stared into the brown eyes that gazed at her so intently. So impatiently. Eyes that demanded a response.

Amanda gave him one. "I lost her."

# CHAPTER FIVE

KIRK BRUSHED past her and strode down the hall.

"Wait!" Amanda ran after him. "That's a restricted area. You can't go there."

"The hell I can't." Kirk didn't break his stride.

"This place is enormous," she called to his back. "You'll never find her on your own."

Kirk stopped and spun around. "Isn't anyone else searching?"

"No—"

Kirk cut her off. "When was the last time you saw Virginia?"

Amanda caught up to him. "When I was talking on the phone with you."

"That was forty-five minutes ago!" He cast her an incredulous look and took off again.

"Kirk..."

He ignored her until he came to the hall leading to the cavernous area behind the studios. Breathing heavily, he put his hands on his hips and stared. "She could be anywhere," he muttered.

"I know," Amanda admitted.

"So what are you doing about it?" he asked sharply.

"Well, I *was* looking for her!"

"How could you let her wander off?"

"I thought she was right outside my office door—"

*"Virginia!"* Kirk bellowed, and began jogging into the cavern, his voice echoing.

"Shh!" Amanda frantically tried to quiet him. "They're filming in the studios. You'll ruin the sound track."

He didn't even bother to respond.

All she could do was run after him. "Kirk, she's got to be in the studio somewhere. Otherwise security would have seen her."

"Is there an intercom system here?" He'd reached the end of the hall and stood looking from right to left as Amanda had earlier.

"I can't use it without authoriz—"

*"I* will then." He stepped toward her, his fury and alarm almost tangible. "My daughter is missing. I'll do whatever it takes to find her."

The time for reasoning had passed. "Let me call my producer." Amanda reached for the in-house phone, grappling for the words to tell Kay that a child was loose in the studios.

"Kay? Amanda. There's a child loose in the studios," she blurted out, deciding to be straightforward.

"Blond hair, blue eyes?"

"Yes!"

"She's here with me."

Amanda sagged against the wall. "They found her," she mouthed to Kirk. "She's fine."

He looked relieved, but no less angry.

"Her father's here," Amanda said. "We'll come get her."

She hung up and faced Kirk. "Virginia is with my executive producer."

"And where is that?"

"This way. C'mon."

As they walked in uncomfortable silence toward Kay's office, Amanda knew she had to say something to the dark-suited man beside her. But what? Did he want reassurance? Groveling? Pleading?

She didn't know him and therefore didn't know what would be the best thing to say. She'd only seen him in suits and blinding white shirts with starched collars and cuffs and subdued ties. His precisely cut hair was swept back from his forehead, completing the look of the consummate successful businessman. Formidable.

And, she might as well admit it, he wasn't hard on the eyes, either.

She inhaled deeply. "I'm sorry."

Kirk said nothing, and for a moment Amanda thought he wouldn't acknowledge her apology. "All this could have been avoided if you'd driven her back to the agency as agreed."

"Or if you'd come to the mall—as agreed." Amanda had already apologized once. One apology per transgression per customer. It was a personal rule.

"I was busy," Kirk informed her.

"So was I," Amanda responded.

They'd reached Kay's office and stopped outside, glaring at each other.

A child's laughter bubbled in the silence.

"That's Virginia." Kirk left Amanda and entered one of the smaller studios. There, seated on a wooden stool, was Virginia, mugging for a camera. She was watching herself on a television monitor.

Kay was operating the camera.

Virginia saw them first. "Daddy!" She wiggled off the stool and came running toward him, arms outflung.

Amanda rolled her eyes.

Kay wandered over to her. "She's okay. Been having a great time." Virginia had obviously uncovered a soft streak in the tough, wiry-haired producer.

"I'll bet." Now that Virginia had been found, Amanda wasn't quite so relieved. In fact, little Miss Virginia was due a scolding.

Apparently she wouldn't be getting it from her father. He'd scooped her up in a big hug, his eyes chastising Amanda over his daughter's shoulder.

"I can't stand this," Amanda grumbled.

"You're using her for the Santa piece?" Kay asked.

Amanda nodded.

"Cute," Kay pronounced. "You should get some good stuff." She glanced over at Amanda. "Might think about expanding the story."

*Expanding?* "Her father isn't too happy right now."

Kay patted Amanda on the arm before returning to her office. "You'll think of something."

"Were you scared, sweetheart?" Kirk asked.

Shaking her head, Virginia slid down from her father's arms and approached Amanda.

Amanda eyed her warily. They both knew that Virginia shouldn't have left the office. But there was no sign of the Virginia who'd mugged for the camera and who'd confidently responded to the interview. Virginia was playing the part of a shy angel.

"I'm sorry, Amanda," she said in a high-pitched voice. "But I had to go to the bathroom."

"I would've taken you," Amanda said.

"But I had to go *bad.*"

Amanda thought back to the giant berry slush. *Thanks a lot, Ron.*

"I got lost," Virginia, with a quick glance at her father, said in the pitiful little voice.

"That's okay, baby. I'm here now," Kirk soothed.

Amanda gazed at Virginia with reluctant admiration. Wow. What a performance. The kid was going to maneuver her way out of any kind of punishment or scolding.

It was past time for Amanda to do a little maneuvering of her own. "Listen, it's late and I was going to order out for pizza. Would you two like to share?"

"Oh, Daddy, please?" Virginia tugged at her immobile father's hand. He didn't refuse immediately, but obviously wanted to.

"While we wait, I'll give you a tour of the studio," Amanda added as another inducement. If they left now, before she made amends, she'd probably never see Virginia again. Or her father.

Kirk checked his watch, but Amanda knew he'd already surrendered. "I suppose so," he agreed, mustering a smile.

Great. All was not lost. "What kind of pizza, Virginia?"

"Pepperoni!"

"Pepperoni it is, then." Too greasy for Amanda's taste, but anything to keep Virginia and her father happy. "I'll make the call."

When she returned, Kirk, Virginia and Kay were watching the tape of Virginia's Santa visit.

Amanda was surprised by a shout of male laughter as the scene of Virginia's struggle with Santa and the elf played.

Kirk looked like a different person when he laughed. Attractive. Younger. Human.

Attractive was the most dangerous. Since she worked in television, Amanda had seen her share of handsome men. In her experience, though, it was the attractive ones you had to watch out for.

The next scene to appear on the monitor was Virginia's interview. Even viewing the rough unedited tape, Amanda could see that Virginia was pretty good.

Kay shared her feelings. Walking backward, the shrewd producer stopped next to Amanda. "The camera loves her."

"And she loves the camera."

Kay regarded the moving images, her hand cupping her chin. "You know, the interview was a brilliant idea."

Amanda felt better.

"Let's *do* expand this into a series."

*"What?"* Amanda's visions of journalistic awards for a child-safety exposé evaporated.

"Sure. We'll tag it onto the afternoon kids' program tomorrow. If it works, we'll offer it to the evening news for their soft portion and run a separate report on each mall Santa."

Amanda wasn't interested in soft news. Amanda wanted hard news. There was more prestige in hard news. Maria Alvarez rarely did soft news anymore. "I've got something better to pitch to you. A series on child safety. Working parents trust others to care for their children, and I've found—"

"Sounds good," Kay interrupted.

Amanda knew better than to take that as an "okay, do it."

"But this is timely," the executive producer continued.

"Child safety is more important," Amanda protested. "I think alerting parents to this problem is more of a service than rating fake Santas."

"'Tis the season to be jolly. Think happy thoughts."
Kay looked up suddenly and caught Amanda's expression. "Play around with it. Be creative." She smiled.
"Then pitch me child safety after the holidays."

It was a start. All Amanda had ever asked for was a
chance.

Virginia's interview ended, and Kay wandered over to
rewind the tape.

"She wasn't bad," Kirk said with an admiring look at
Virginia.

"She was really good," Amanda admitted. Virginia's
overdone antics translated into a bright peppiness that
would appeal to children and their parents. Amanda
might not want to be doing this particular story, but it
would be a lot worse without Virginia. "We should have
just enough time for a quick tour before the pizza ar-
rives."

Dinner was surprisingly enjoyable. When Kirk wasn't
angry or in a hurry, he was a decent human being—and
that was saying a lot for a man, in Amanda's opinion.

They ate in Amanda's cramped office. Virginia chat-
tered on and on about her visit to the mall. Amanda let
her. She wanted Kirk to see just how important the Santa
visits were to his daughter—especially now that Kay
wanted them expanded.

"Do you often eat here?" Kirk asked when Virginia's
mouth was full of pepperoni pizza.

"More than I should. Why?"

Kirk grinned. "The delivery boy called you by name."

Quite a few delivery boys called her by name. She decided not to tell him the delivery man at the kolache shop
not only knew her name, but had a standing morning
order for one apricot kolache and a large coffee. Shrug-
ging, she took a piece of pizza she didn't really want. "I

spend a lot of time here, depending on what's in production." Then she confessed, "And something's *always* in production."

"How does your family feel about that?"

Amanda bit into her pizza. He was really asking if she was married. She'd been single long enough to know the code. She'd also been single long enough to know how to answer evasively if she chose. She didn't choose. "I live alone. Not even a cat."

Amanda glanced at him as she answered and caught a spark of interest in his eyes.

"We live alone, too," Virginia offered. "Except sometimes Mrs. Webster stays over."

"The housekeeper," Kirk added.

Amanda already knew he was a widower, but it didn't sound as though he was currently involved with anyone other than Virginia and Mrs. Webster.

She thought about that little spark. Was there a little spark in her, too? Maybe a tiny glowing ember left from the smoldering anger?

He was attractive, outwardly well-to-do, eligible . . .

And a father. Kirk bent his dark head next to Virginia's blond one. Taking a paper napkin with the Luciano's Pizza logo on it, he carefully wiped a smear of tomato sauce from her cheek.

Amanda tossed her half-eaten slice of pizza into the box lid. Kirk McEnery had responsibilities—the sort of responsibilities Amanda had avoided ever since her disastrous marriage.

But Kirk McEnery's responsibilities were hardly her business. She was certainly presuming a lot from one look of interest, wasn't she?

Then again, maybe not. Her hand brushed Kirk's as she reached for a napkin for herself. Startled at the contact, she jerked back, then glanced up to see if he'd noticed.

He had. Those brown eyes were definitely sizing her up.

Amanda couldn't look away, even when Virginia giggled.

Wearing an infinitesimal smile, Kirk reached for a napkin. "Here."

To Amanda's surprise, then embarrassment, he touched the napkin to a corner of her mouth. She grabbed the napkin from him and scrubbed at her lips. "Uh, thanks," she mumbled, feeling her face flame. Wonderful. She hadn't blushed since she was a kid.

"You're welcome. I've had a lot of experience," he said easily, grinning in response to her surprised expression.

"Well." She crumbled the napkin and dropped it on top of her discarded pizza. "There's one piece left. Virginia?"

The little girl shook her head, her speculative gaze darting from her father to Amanda.

"Ready to go home?" Kirk asked Virginia.

"Will I get to visit more Santas?" she asked, taking his hand.

"That's up to Ms. Donnelly."

Amanda breathed a prayer of thanks. "I'm willing to go out again tomorrow."

Kirk frowned. "I've got a couple in from out of town. They've been transferred to Houston and need a home. I'll be busy with them all day."

*Of course you will.* "I'll be happy to drive Virginia," Amanda said, trying to sound as though she meant it.

WHEN AMANDA APPROACHED the circular drive in front of Cameron Elementary, she felt like an old pro. This time Mrs. Hull recognized her, and Virginia bounced into the car.

"Guess what?" she said, slamming the door. "I'm going to be in the Christmas pageant!"

"Great!" Amanda said, trying to dodge stray children.

"I've never been in a pageant before."

"What part do you play?"

"I don't know. We're doing Christmas around the World. Mrs. Woods—she's the music teacher—said I was going to get a speaking part!"

"Well, congratulations."

"Mrs. Woods said we'll have to work really hard to be ready in time. We can't miss any rehearsals," Virginia said, obviously quoting.

Rehearsals. "Gosh, I hope the rehearsals don't interfere with our Santa tapings," Amanda said without thinking. "When is the program?"

"The third Tuesday night in December."

Virginia spoke with such uncharacteristic reserve that Amanda took her eyes off the road and glanced at her. The little girl gripped the strap of her backpack so tightly her knuckles were white.

Amanda felt horrible. "It'll be okay. We'll just have to work around your rehearsals." Inwardly she groaned. "We do it all the time with the big stars. That's what I get for choosing someone as talented as you are."

Virginia visibly relaxed, reminding Amanda that for all her bravado, she was really a vulnerable child. "I'll get to wear a costume and everything. Maybe even makeup," Virginia added slyly.

The old Virginia was back. Amanda was glad. "And just where do you think you're going to get makeup, young lady?"

"From you."

"Oh, yeah?"

"Yeah!" Virginia dissolved into giggles.

"What do you think your father will say?"

Still laughing, Virginia responded. "Oh, he won't notice. He's too busy."

Though Virginia didn't seem upset, Amanda felt a pang. A father too busy to notice makeup on his six-year-old daughter?

"He's not that busy." Amanda found herself hoping it was true. But Virginia shook her head.

*It's none of your business,* Amanda told herself, then repeated it for good measure. "What do your friends think about your being on television?"

"They don't believe me." It didn't sound as if that was unusual.

"I guess you'll show them, huh?"

"Yeah. Where are we going today?"

"We're going to check out the Santa at Willowwood Mall. Have you ever shopped at that mall?"

"I don't know," Virginia answered, wrinkling her forehead as she tried to remember. "Will Ron be there?"

"Why? So you can talk him into another berry slush?"

Virginia grinned. "Yeah."

"Ha." Amanda remembered what happened after the last berry slush. "Not this time, kiddo."

"THE SLUSHES at Willowwood Mall are better than the ones at Woodbrook," Virginia pronounced after slurping all the way back to the studio.

"Let's make a stop in the ladies' room before we go to my office," Amanda said, taking the empty cup and discarding it. With a stern look, she led Virginia in the direction of the public rest rooms next to the security guard.

When they came out, Amanda was astonished to see Kirk waiting by the guard's station.

"What are you doing here?" Amanda blurted out as he settled a hand on Virginia's shoulder.

Kirk raised an eyebrow. "I came to pick up Virginia," he said, but his gaze settled on Amanda.

"I knew that, I just meant..." Amanda fluffed her bangs. "We were going to watch the broadcast with Virginia's first Santa report. You don't want to miss that, do you?"

Chuckling, Kirk admitted, "I've got my VCR set to record it, but we've got time to stay and watch it here if that's all right with you." He was still smiling and looking quite unhurried.

"S-sure," she stuttered. *Get a grip!* She pointed to the sofas in the waiting area. Multiple monitors hung just below the ceiling.

"Did you sell that couple a house?" Amanda asked as they waited for Virginia's segment to appear.

Kirk hesitated a moment before answering. "They've narrowed their choices to three and wanted to talk it over during dinner, then take another look."

"So when do you have to be back?" Amanda was conscious that Virginia had gone very quiet.

Kirk must have noticed, as well. Putting an arm around Virginia, he settled into the sofa. "I... turned them over to one of the other brokers."

That didn't sound like the Kirk McEnery Amanda knew. "Why?"

She didn't think he was going to answer. "She hasn't had a sale all month," he said, as if giving away part of a commission was no big deal.

"That's very—"

He interrupted her to point at the monitor. "There's Virginia!"

Even though Amanda had spent the day viewing the tape with the video editor, she saw it again through Kirk's and Virginia's eyes and knew it was a good piece.

The instant Virginia saw herself, she giggled, groaned, then covered her face with her hands. "I still sound funny!" She turned around to see what Amanda and her father thought.

Kirk held a finger up to his lips.

After Virginia got used to seeing herself, she watched the rest of the segment with an embarrassed grin.

After it was over, Virginia was trying to wheedle pepperoni pizza out of Amanda when the security guard motioned to her and handed her the telephone.

"Amanda—is the kid still there?"

"Yes, Kay."

"Bring her back to studio C. The switchboard's lighting up."

"People are calling about Virginia's Santa-rating already?" People were weird sometimes.

"I told you—they love this stuff during the holidays. We're running it again at the end of the six-o'clock news. Hurry."

Amanda didn't even get a chance to ask what Kay wanted. Fortunately Kirk was still in an amiable mood and didn't protest. When they reached studio C, Kay was waiting for them.

"Virginia, can you read?" Kay thrust her scribbled notes at the girl and conferred with the camera crew.

"*I* can't even read your writing," Amanda said, looking over Virginia's shoulder.

As soon as she figured out what Kay wanted Virginia to say, Amanda explained, "On a scale of one to ten, with ten being the real Santa, what number would you give the guy at Woodbrook?"

"I don't understand," Virginia said.

Kay motioned for them to hurry.

"How much money would you pay to see that Santa?" Kirk asked. "The better the Santa, the more money he costs."

*That's right, reduce everything to money,* Amanda criticized silently.

"I wouldn't pay anything. He wasn't worth it."

"He was better than nothing," Amanda said.

"If you won't pay money, then something else," Kirk suggested. "How about candy canes?"

"Ohh, that's good," Kay murmured. "A candy-cane rating."

"Do I have to?" Virginia asked. "I like candy canes. I didn't like that guy. He smelled."

"Yes, you have to." Amanda positioned Virginia in front of a blue screen.

"Okay, three, then. But no more."

Once that was established, Amanda prompted Virginia, and they painstakingly taped a few more seconds to be used with the evening news, then Kay whisked the tape off to editing.

"A lot of work goes into taping," Kirk commented.

Was that admiration she heard? "Yes. And it looks as though there will be a lot more ahead of us. We still have half-a-dozen malls to visit. Tomorrow's Saturday,'' Amanda said. "Could Virginia and I make a day of it?''

"Sounds fine.'' Kirk retrieved his daughter, who was trying to climb up the camera dolly to look through the viewfinder. "I'll come with you.''

# CHAPTER SIX

IF AMANDA HADN'T SEEN them with her own eyes, she'd never have believed it. There, coming toward her from the north parking-lot entrance, was Kirk McEnery, leading Virginia by the hand.

And they were three minutes early.

Amanda swallowed. Kirk wore a pullover sweater with a sophisticated geometric design and classic, but casual pants. He was clearly off duty.

And on a Saturday, too. Amanda couldn't believe Kirk had forced himself to take the time.

"Amanda! Look at me! Look at me!" Virginia dropped Kirk's hand and tugged at her green sweatshirt. "Mrs. Webster painted it. Isn't it cool?"

Glittering candy canes and Santa Clauses adorned Virginia's front and back.

"It's perfect!" Amanda slowly walked around the excited little girl. "Santa's beard is even fuzzy."

"And I have bells." Virginia jumped up and down to demonstrate.

"Mrs. Webster is very talented." Amanda glanced up at Kirk to find him gazing at Virginia with undisguised love.

Something about his expression reached right inside Amanda, grabbed her long-buried maternal instinct and gave it a good yank.

"She and Virginia worked on it last night after we got home," he said.

Virginia traced one of the red-and-white candy canes. "The candy canes are for the candy-cane ratings."

Amanda saluted the creative Mrs. Webster. "And what are the bells for?"

"So you won't lose me," Virginia explained just as she darted over to look into a store window.

"Your Mrs. Webster sounds like a real gem," Amanda commented.

"She is." Kirk touched Amanda's arm to guide her toward Virginia, who had already abandoned the first store and crisscrossed to the other side of the mall. "So far, she's stayed with us longer than any other housekeeper."

"Have you had a lot of housekeepers?"

"Yes." He spoke with such feeling that Amanda waited for him to explain.

He saw her questioning look and obliged. "Virginia's nanny quit the day Michelle and I arrived home from our honeymoon. We've had a string of housekeepers ever since. Virginia!" She'd turned the wrong way, and Kirk motioned for her to join them.

Amanda mulled over his last statement. People generally didn't have a need for nannies when they took honeymoons.

"I see Ron!" Virginia raced past them, a jingling blur of green.

Kirk chuckled. "Going at things full tilt, just like her mother always did."

Amanda didn't know how to react. She was curious to know the whole story but didn't want to pry. Her silence drew Kirk's attention, and he correctly interpreted her unasked questions.

"Virginia was about eighteen months old when I married Michelle. It was a package deal." He lifted a corner of his mouth. "And I got the bargain."

"So Virginia isn't..." Halfway into the question, Amanda wished she hadn't opened her mouth. Technicalities weren't important.

"She is," Kirk stated. "I adopted her."

Both he and Amanda watched as the little dynamo reached for Ron's hand and urged him toward the food court. Ron shook his head, but Virginia obviously wasn't taking no for an answer.

"And it's been quite an adventure," Kirk added quietly.

Amanda was bombarded by a variety of emotions. She immediately wondered about Virginia's biological father, but knew better than to ask. And then she wondered why she was so curious about Kirk and his daughter. Sure, the little girl was a charmer, but Amanda had met lots of charmers. And Kirk was consuming far more of her mental energy than anyone had in a long time. "We..." Amanda had to stop and clear her throat. "We better rescue Ron."

As they walked toward what appeared to be Santa's oasis in the Adobe South Mall, she continued to wonder about Virginia's mother, wondered how and when she'd died.

But those questions would have to wait for another time. Right now, Amanda had a story to tape.

The Adobe South Mall Santa had a decidedly Spanish flair. Palm trees, of all things, circled the scene. Luminarios, paper bags with sand and an electric candle inside, lit the path to Santa's throne. His house, in this version, resembled a stable, perhaps an oblique reference to the nativity. The peppy "Feliz Navidad" serenaded them. According to the sign, when Santa was gone, he wasn't feeding his reindeer, he was taking a siesta.

Since the mall had just opened for the day, the line to see Santa wasn't very long, and Amanda wanted to take advantage of the lull.

Ron had already set up. Virginia was prompted, then Kirk and Amanda stepped back and let her talk to Santa.

"Ho-ho-ho!" boomed Santa.

Amanda watched closely for Virginia's reaction. This Santa had a white beard—and a black mustache.

Virginia didn't tug on the beard.

The elves, once they ascertained that Kirk didn't want a photograph, melted into the background. Amanda was grateful and impressed.

"You been a good leetle girl all the time?"

Virginia nodded.

"Ah—" Santa held up a white-gloved finger "—tell Santa the truth."

Virginia looked scared.

Santa draped his arm around her. "Ho-ho. 'Course you haven't been good *all* the time. *Nobody* is good *all* the time—not even Santa!"

"Really?" Virginia asked in a small hopeful voice.

"For sure. You just gotta be good *most* of the time. Are you?"

"I try," Virginia said earnestly.

"That's all Santa asks. Now, you got somethin' you wanna ask Santa?"

"Could I have a Super Nintendo for Christmas?"

"You want a Super Nintendo for Christmas?" Santa repeated loudly, obviously alerting any interested parties of Virginia's Christmas wish. "Say, you want Super Mario Brothers with that?"

Wordlessly, Virginia nodded.

"Anything else? Another game controller? You got brothers and sisters you can share with?"

Eyes wide, Virginia leaned close and whispered into Santa's ear.

He gave her a gentle smile and patted her on the shoulder. "Santa will do his best. For now, looky what I got here for you." He picked up a basket and indicated that Virginia should select something from it.

She picked her gift, hopped off his lap and headed for Amanda.

What had Virginia whispered to him? Amanda wondered.

"I got a coin purse." Virginia held up a pink plastic object, then began to play with the zipper.

"You did a good job," Amanda said, motioning to Kirk.

He'd stayed well out of the way during the taping. Amanda had been conscious of him, but had concentrated on Virginia and Santa.

"He's great with kids," Kirk murmured in an aside to Amanda.

Amanda nodded to show that she'd heard him, then turned to Virginia, who was still fascinated by the zipper on her new coin purse. "Let's go sit down somewhere and fill out our rating sheet."

"I'm thirsty," Virginia announced.

"What do you want, honey?" Kirk asked.

"A slush." Virginia began bouncing and jingling toward the food court.

"Care to join us?" he asked Amanda.

"I don't know." She pretended to hesitate. "A slush isn't very nutritious."

Kirk looked blank for a moment, then gave her a sheepish grin. "I suppose it wouldn't hurt just this once."

Over two regular berry slushes and one super-duper triple-strength berry slush, Amanda and Virginia rated the Adobe South Santa.

"Seven candy canes is a lot," Amanda cautioned. It was a little too early to declare the perfect Santa.

"He gets seven candy canes," Virginia insisted, her lips purple. "Maybe eight. Or maybe all of them if he passes the test."

"What test?" Amanda hoped the stain on Virginia's mouth would wear off before the next taping. After that, it was agreed that the crew would leave them to tape a bit of each mall Santa. Amanda, Virginia and Kirk would be on their own to visit the Santas at a slower pace.

"My secret Santa test. It's the way I'll know he's real." Virginia grinned, showing her purple gums and tongue. Did that mean Amanda's tongue was purple, too? She looked at Kirk, but he wasn't opening his mouth.

"When will you know if he passes the test?" Amanda asked.

"Christmas."

"Can you make it Christmas Eve?"

Virginia's brows drew together. "I don't know." She looked from her father to Amanda.

"Kay—you remember Kay?"

Virginia nodded.

"Kay wants us to choose the best Santa and announce him on Christmas Eve." A thought occurred to her. "You all aren't going out of town for the holidays, are you?"

"Not this year," Kirk answered. "What would you give this Santa if he didn't pass the test?" he asked Virginia.

"Seven, no eight candy canes."

"Why?" Amanda asked, surprised at the same answer.

"I liked his voice and his boots were big and black. He had a soft lap, too."

"But?" Amanda prompted.

"Well...I don't *think* he was the real Santa. The white part of his beard wasn't real, but his mustache was."

"Maybe Santa got tired of his beard and shaved it off," Kirk suggested. "But since everyone expects him to have a beard, he has to wear a fake one." Kirk looked pleased with his explanation.

Amanda glared at him.

Virginia chewed on her straw. "Maybe. But he was nice and I like my purse."

"Okay, eight candy canes it is," Amanda said, before Kirk could jump in with any more wild theories.

"Where to next?" he asked, looking miffed.

"Buffalo Bayou Mall."

Houston's largest and richest mall was known for its spectacular holiday decorations. Amanda had no doubt Santa Claus would be properly enshrined.

And he was. Virginia approached the center of the mall and tilted her head back, gazing to the very top of a huge green Christmas tree. The base was on the ground floor of the mall, and the top ended just under the skylights three levels above. Thousands of tiny white lights twinkled in its branches.

Running in a loop along the center of the mall was a train track manned by mechanical elves. A toy train chugged through one elaborate scene after another. At the very end of the mall reigned the great man himself.

Virginia was apparently struck dumb by the magnificent splendor of Santa's kingdom.

Even Amanda found it difficult to maintain her cynicism when faced with such an opulent rendering. "I feel like I've stepped into a Christmas television special," she said.

"Isn't that what you're taping?" Kirk asked.

"You know what I mean." She followed Virginia, who had gone to the railing around the Christmas tree. "This must have cost a fortune."

"But if it brings people into the mall, it's worth it, don't you agree?" Kirk steadied Virginia as she stepped onto the support bar and leaned over as far as she could, reaching toward the tree.

"Only if they spend money."

"That's the idea."

Virginia stretched, but couldn't quite touch the tree.

"Oh, I know the routine." Amanda gestured to the expensive stores surrounding them. "Spend, give, get, return."

Kirk raised an eyebrow. "A little early for seasonal burnout, isn't it?"

"Don't mind me—I'm permanently burned out." Yet, she followed the progress of the train as it rolled in and out of sparkling foam igloos. Virginia quietly stared at the tree.

"Is Christmas too commercial for you?" Kirk asked with a touch of sarcasm in his voice.

Why was Kirk pursuing this? "They can commercialize it all they want. I just don't like Christmas."

"Do you think everyone should forget all this once-a-year generosity and get back to the religion?" Kirk crossed his arms over his chest. He was getting ready to cry hypocrite, Amanda guessed.

She didn't want to discuss Christmas with him. "Religion *is* the point of the holiday, and a little religious guilt never hurt anybody." With that, she hooked an arm around Virginia's waist and pried the little girl from the railing. "Time to visit Santa."

The line to see Santa stretched through two train stops. Amanda tried to facilitate matters by breaking into the line.

"The end of the line's back there," a rigid-jawed mother informed her.

"Well, yes, but I'm—"

"Is there a problem?" A roving elf materialized beside them.

"She was trying to break into line," the mother accused Amanda, accompanied by murmuring agreement from those in the vicinity.

"Breaking into line is cause for ejection from the mall," the elf said in a voice intended to sound pleasant and reasonable with a don't-let-these-pointy-toed-shoes-fool-you firmness.

Amanda put on her wide associate-producer smile. "I'm Amanda Donnelly with 'Hello Houston.'" She thrust out her hand and the elf shook it, though she looked as though she'd rather not. "We're taping a segment on visiting Santa Claus. Now if I could just put Virginia here—" Amanda pulled Virginia toward the line "—we'll only take a minute. And your child will probably be in some of the shots," she said to the mother.

The woman shoved her stroller, cutting off Virginia and clipping Amanda's ankle. Amanda gasped.

"You can break in somewhere else. I've been standing in this line for over half an hour."

"We're taping—"

"So am I!" Another parent held up a video camera. "Now, take a hike."

So much for peace on earth, goodwill toward associate producers. With the elf firmly grabbing her elbow, Amanda tried one more time. "Look—there's my camera crew." She pointed to Ron and the lighting tech.

"Some parents make such a production out of everything," one woman commented to another as the elf, now reinforced by a security guard, pulled Amanda away.

"I watch 'Hello Houston,'" said a man farther down the line. "Maria Alvarez is on 'Hello Houston.'" Pointing to Amanda, he continued, "*She's* not Maria Alvarez."

*Maria Alvarez, always Maria Alvarez.* Amanda bet Maria Alvarez had never been dragged off by an elf. "We'll wait at the end of the line," Amanda said, snatching her elbow from the elf's grasp.

Burning with humiliation, she motioned for Ron to stay put and gestured for Kirk and Virginia to join her.

Kirk hadn't said anything, though his lips quivered suspiciously. Amanda wished he'd comment and get it over with. Or laugh the way she could tell he wanted to. "Gee, thanks for your help," she muttered finally.

"You know you'd hate it if I played white knight," he said, seemingly unperturbed.

It didn't help Amanda's mood to realize that he was absolutely right. "I wouldn't have hated it right then." She grimaced. "Maybe later."

His grin breaking through at last, Kirk withdrew his wallet. Extracting a bill, he whispered in Virginia's ear, then pointed toward a candy store a few steps away.

"Sure!" Virginia jingled over to the counter and pressed her face against the chocolate bins.

"What did you do that for?" Amanda protested. "She might get chocolate all over her outfit."

Kirk just smiled. Amanda had seen that smile before.

Men smiled that way when they were feeling superior and women were being illogical and emotional. "The chocolate is for you."

"Why?"

"Thought it would help." He still wore that smug smile. "The agency goes through pounds of M&M's each week, depending on the activity in the Houston real-estate market."

Amanda felt she should make an objection. But as her gaze slid sideways toward the chocolate shop, her heart wasn't in it. "Virginia!" Amanda pointed. "The chocolate-covered cashews... Yes, over there."

She heard Kirk laugh and reluctantly allowed her face to relax. "Okay, maybe just this once."

"I've heard that before."

"No, really. I don't eat chocolate when I'm stressed." Amanda dug in her pocket for her worry stone. "Look. I carry this with me." She placed the smooth white-veined rock in his palm.

As he rubbed his thumb back and forth across the indentation, Amanda wondered at herself. She'd never told anyone about her worry stones, not even Kay.

"I used to have one of these," Kirk was saying. "This has got a good weight." He jiggled it up and down and handed it back to Amanda as Virginia skipped back toward them.

"You haven't moved very much," she complained.

"I know. It'll take us at least half an hour." Amanda reached for the white bag Virginia held. "Let's see, let's see."

"You didn't get very many," Virginia said, opening the bag and taking out a big, swirled, multicolored sucker.

"Is that a weapon?" Amanda asked, and then bit into a chocolate-covered cashew. Wonderful. She chewed, feeling better already.

Belatedly, and with a mouth full of chocolate, she offered the bag to Kirk.

Looking every inch the smug superior male, he declined. "Maybe later."

Ha. He actually thought there would be chocolate left over. Amanda popped the rest of her piece into her mouth. Men *didn't* know everything.

After an excruciating forty-minute wait and a trip to the rest room, Virginia had her Santa visit.

To Amanda, he looked like a movie Santa Claus. As children and parents approached, a hush fell over the crowd. Magic was in the air. Christmas magic.

"He might be real," Virginia insisted afterward, as she ate a corn dog and drank lemonade in the food court. "If he passes my test, then I'll know he is."

"What test is that?" Kirk asked.

"Not going to tell." And she didn't, even though both Kirk and Amanda tried tricks and bribes.

The Buffalo Bayou Santa received a nine-candy-cane rating, the ten rating being reserved for the *real* Santa as determined by Virginia.

They said goodbye to the crew, who could tape much faster without waiting for Virginia to work her way through the lines.

No other Santa quite matched up to the Buffalo Bayou Santa. At Providence Mall, Santa was high tech and when he was on a break, he was "entering data into his computer."

At Riceland Mall, Santa was an ecologist and cautioned each child to help save the earth. He wore no fur on his red-velvet outfit, and his toes peeked out of sandals made of recycled automobile tires. This Santa turned down Virginia's request for a Super Nintendo and offered a hand-carved, wooden whale puzzle, instead. Virginia was unimpressed, even when Santa pointed out that a portion of the proceeds would be donated to saving the whales. This Santa rated no candy canes in her opinion.

When Amanda balked at this, Kirk disagreed. "Kids don't want a lecture on the environment. They just want to see Santa."

"Well, how do we know that he *isn't* Santa?" Amanda argued. Only when Kirk's expression registered did she realize what she'd said.

Gulf Shores Mall rivaled Adobe South for most bizarre mix of traditional Christmas decorations and mall theme.

Santa, in full regalia—Virginia thought it was actually the best costume of the lot—sat in a thatched beach hut. Real sand and fluorescent-colored conch shells added to the ambience. His elves were hula dancers with floral leis, and Virginia received a yellow plastic lei as her Santa treat.

"I'm hungry," she announced.

"I'm not surprised," murmured her father.

"The food court is that way." Amanda pointed. "And the telephones are this way. I want to call the studio."

The mall was crowded and noisy with holiday shoppers. A long line of teenagers waited for the telephones. Amanda fidgeted with a quarter and glared at the girl using the phone ahead of her. The girl turned away, her permed ponytail nearly catching Amanda in the face.

An eternity later, Amanda shoved her quarter into the slot and plugged her ear with her finger. "Back off, will you?" she said to the teenager behind her.

"What?" asked a voice in the receiver.

"Kay!"

"I've seen Ron's tape from this morning," the producer said as soon as Amanda identified herself. "What's the kid whispering?"

"She won't tell us. She insists that it's her test for the real Santa."

"She thinks the big guy's out there somewhere, huh?"

"Apparently so."

"How will she know which one comes through for her?"

"I've no idea." Amanda remembered Virginia's resolute face as she talked with each Santa. "I just hope she's not disappointed."

"I think it's a great gimmick."

"Kay—" Amanda hesitated "—to Virginia, this is all real. I don't want her to get hurt."

"Then find out what she wants and make sure she gets it."

"Wait a minute—*I'm* not Santa."

"You may have to be." Kay chuckled. "Can you bring Virginia back here to tape the ratings?"

Amanda winced. "It's getting late and we're tired and full of mall food."

"Tomorrow, then. We'll start running these on Monday."

Would this story never end? Amanda wondered as she found Kirk and Virginia eating pizza.

"Amanda, we saved you the one with the most pepperoni on it." Virginia pulled a wad of napkins from the metal dispenser and dropped them at Amanda's place.

Amanda mustered a smile. "Thanks."

"You'll note that it's the *only* one left," Kirk pointed out. "If you want more, I—"

"No! No more." Amanda covered her eyes with her hands, to Virginia's giggling delight. "We've been eating all day long."

"It's been an awesome day. Where do we go next?" Virginia asked, eyeing Amanda's pizza.

"That's up to your dad. Bellaire Mall is the only other mall within the city limits." She looked at Kirk. It would be dark outside by now, and it *had* been a long day.

"Please, Daddy?" Virginia bounced on the white stool. "I'm not tired."

"Yes, I can see that," Kirk responded dryly. "Okay, one more mall and then we're done."

"Except for taping the candy-cane rating back at the studio," Amanda slipped in.

"What?" Kirk looked like a man at the end of his rope.

"Which we can do tomorrow," she added hastily.

They actually sang Christmas carols as they made the long drive from Gulf Shores Mall to Bellaire Mall. Amanda had parked her car back at the first mall, and she'd enjoyed being a passenger for once.

Kirk's car was a large, late-model American luxury car. He'd responded to Amanda's raised eyebrows with a nod toward the odometer. "I use this car to drive clients all over Houston."

Amanda blinked twice at the high mileage.

"Buying a house is stressful and I want them to be able to relax and think," Kirk said, opening the door for her.

Amanda remembered that now, while the car hummed along the freeway, cushioning them from bumps and noise.

She could get used to this sort of luxury.

"What can we get to eat at this mall?" Virginia asked as they pulled into the well-lit parking lot.

"Try something from the vegetable food group," Kirk told her. "You haven't had any fruit or vegetables all day long."

"I have, too! I drink berry slushes—that's fruit."

"So, what about a vegetable?" Amanda took sides with Kirk. It felt rather domestic.

"Pickles. They're a vegetable."

"No, they aren't," Amanda denied automatically.

"They're made out of cucumbers," Virginia said with a self-righteous air. "Cucumbers are vegetables."

"But—"

"She'll be all right." Kirk put a hand on Amanda's shoulder and leaned close, murmuring in her ear. "This is one argument you won't win."

Amanda, jolted by his touch, barely heard him. It was meant to be an impersonal touch, she knew, but that wasn't the way her body reacted to it.

She wanted to be touched again. By him. And soon. As a matter of fact, she—Amanda Donnelly, independent woman—wanted to nestle, yes, nestle, against him. Not only that, out of her own mouth, she'd heard words that sounded suspiciously parental.

The malls were obviously piping something through the air-filtering systems. Either that, or they were putting something in the food. *Subliminal Advertising: How far will they go?*

Amanda sniffed as they entered Bellaire Mall.

With the self-confidence of a veteran Santa Sleuth, Virginia marched toward Santa's workshop.

A low-key traditional display, it was actually Amanda's personal favorite. There was none of the awe connected with the Buffalo Bayou Santa. When Santa was on his break, he was "in his workshop, overseeing the elves."

"Fake snow," Virginia announced, grabbing a handful and tossing it into the air.

"Virginia!" Both Kirk and Amanda chastised her in unison.

Kirk smiled down at her. "You're getting the hang of this parenting business."

Virginia took her place in line as Amanda's answering smile wavered.

*Parenting business.* It had been years since she'd thought about having a child. A child had been out of the question during her brief marriage. Even more so after it.

Now she didn't have time for a child. She had goals, and a child would take away from her goals. In fact, Amanda's last promotion had occurred during Maria Alvarez's maternity leave. And Maria hadn't had a promotion in a long while. She'd cut back on her work hours to spend more time with her baby.

Amanda couldn't afford to do that now. She had enough lost time to make up for.

When it was Virginia's turn, a male elf—the first male elf Amanda had seen—approached them. "Would you two like to get in the picture with your daughter?"

"Oh, we're not—" Amanda started to say, but to her surprise, Kirk grabbed her elbow.

"Yes. We *would* like one of us all together." He urged her toward Virginia and Santa Claus.

"Kirk! You don't want me in the picture."

"Yes, I do." He looked down at her, his eyes dark. "I've enjoyed today, and I'd like a memento."

Amanda didn't know what to say. "But I'm a mess." She fluffed her bangs nervously.

"Not to me," he said in a low voice.

Amanda stared at him, trying to fathom his expression. Was he simply caught up in the "spirit of Christmas"? Poisoned by too much mall food?

"How many copies?" asked the elf.

"One," answered Kirk as he turned toward the camera.

She caught the look he gave Virginia and the girl's adoring one in return. Virginia was thrilled, and she beamed at the camera.

Amanda's eyes stung and suddenly she heard herself say, "Make that *two* copies."

# CHAPTER SEVEN

AMANDA FELT a pang of regret as she directed Kirk to her parked car in the Adobe South Mall lot. She wasn't ready for the day to end. It had been more a day of companionship and pleasure than one of work. Most of Amanda's days were workdays. Even when she technically had a day off, she found herself stopping by the studio.

Amanda couldn't remember the last time she'd simply frittered time away with friends.

Come to think of it, other than her co-workers, did she still *have* any friends?

Kirk parked his car behind hers, left the engine running and got out to open her door.

"I want to sit up front now," Virginia said with a yawn. She climbed from the rear seat and gave Amanda a sleepy hug. "'Bye, Amanda."

"'Bye, Virginia." Amanda felt oddly touched. She hugged the little girl back, and to her surprise, Virginia responded by kissing her on the cheek.

Flustered, Amanda tried to cover her awkward feelings by fastening Virginia's seat belt before straightening and facing Kirk.

She would've given anything to know what he was thinking at that moment. His face was expressionless, but his eyes held a vulnerability she hadn't expected.

Her hand shook as she fitted the key into her car door. "Thanks for coming today," she said, trying to fill the too-intimate silence with words. "I noticed that Virginia seemed very natural in front of the camera and was more patient waiting in line than I was. I'm sure your being there had a lot to do with it."

"I enjoyed the day, as well," Kirk said quietly. "I don't get a chance to spend much time with Virginia."

He didn't *make* many chances to spend time with Virginia, Amanda said to herself, then felt guilty. He was a single parent—how could she possibly know what that was like?

They looked at the little girl, who had fallen asleep.

"'Bye, Kirk," Amanda said in a whimsical imitation of Virginia.

"'Bye, Amanda," he echoed.

At the exact instant Amanda would have turned to sit in her car, Kirk bent his head.

*I hope he doesn't think I expected to be kissed,* was her embarrassed thought as she instinctively turned her cheek toward him.

Kirk must have been aiming for her cheek because his kiss landed squarely on her lips.

They parted abruptly and then laughed at the awkwardness.

Then, just as Amanda stepped back, Kirk placed both hands on either side of her face, holding her still.

Their laughter died.

Amanda was lost in the brown depths of his eyes. His head descended slowly, forcing her to realize that he intended to kiss her, and if she didn't want him to, she had ample time to pull away.

Not only did Amanda not pull away, she leaned toward him, drawn by a compelling need to know his touch.

Kirk's lips met hers in a very definite kiss with a very definite thoroughness—which created very definite longings within her.

His hands were warm against her face, and she felt cherished and protected, even standing in the parking lot under the pink halogen security lights.

He broke the kiss slowly, as slowly as he'd begun it. "Good night, Amanda," he whispered, and stepped back, drawing his hands away with a final caress.

Amanda was able to get into her car and start the engine only because she knew he'd wait there until he was certain she was safely on her way.

But Amanda didn't feel safe. As she drove off, she was very much afraid that she was leaving a piece of her heart behind.

"AMANDA!" KAY SNAPPED her fingers. "Did you hear me?"

"Uh, yes." Amanda focused her wandering attention.

"Humble and Kingwood malls want their Santas rated."

"Can the kid do it?"

"I don't know."

"*Amanda*. You're supposed to say, 'Sure, Kay, I'll get right on it.' "

"She's in a Christmas pageant." But telling Kay about the pageant was only a stalling tactic Amanda used while she decided if she wanted to see Kirk and Virginia again.

His kiss had thoroughly rattled her. Worse, it had made her dissatisfied with her life, reminded her what she'd been missing. It wasn't fair. For years she'd worked toward her goal of becoming a full producer, with an eye on senior producer, then executive producer—the top position. Then maybe making the jump to network television. She'd allowed friendships to wither and her life to revolve around her work. Until now, she hadn't particularly minded. Why should one kiss change all that?

Amanda wasn't certain she wanted to find out.

She hadn't seen Kirk since Saturday night. Mrs. Webster had driven Virginia to the studio the next afternoon, making pointed remarks about people who worked on Sundays. Amanda was both relieved and disappointed not to face Kirk again.

Even though she had a legitimate reason, it was only Kay's prodding that made Amanda dial Kirk McEnery's agency now.

"Kirk McEnery."

When did he start answering his own telephone? "Hi. It's Amanda." *Oh, that sounded real professional.*

"Hello, Amanda." Kirk's voice instantly warmed.

"I wanted to talk to you about Virginia," she blurted out.

"What about Virginia?" he asked amiably.

"Um..." She should've thought about what to say before phoning him. This was awful. He hadn't called her; he probably thought she was chasing him. Well, so what? She was an independent woman. If she wanted to chase, she should be able to chase.

But she wasn't chasing. In fact, she had begun to wonder why *he* wasn't chasing.

"Are you there?" he asked.

Amanda rustled some papers on her desk. "Yes, sorry. Someone just put something in front of me." Loosely covering the receiver, she pretended to speak to someone in her office, "I'll be with you in a minute." Removing her hand from the telephone, she apologized again. "Sorry about that."

"Busy day?"

"Aren't they all?" Amanda laughed even as she made a face. Reduced to playing games. How humiliating.

"Too busy for lunch?"

Amanda's mouth fell open. "Lunch? I... Sure." She stared down at her black vest and pants. She wasn't dressed for a ritzy lunch date, and she knew Kirk would be faultlessly attired as usual.

"Good. I'll come to your side of town. Know any good parks?"

"Parks?"

"Where we can eat," he explained with no hint of impatience. "Have you been outside lately?"

Actually, Amanda was rarely outside. "I drove to work this morning. I could hardly see."

"The fog has lifted, and the sun is out. This has turned into one of those days nature gives Houston to apologize for August."

Was this lighthearted man the same Kirk McEnery she'd encountered before? He'd probably just earned a big fat commission.

"It's a day for picnicking in the park. Are you game?"

"A picnic!" His enthusiasm finally got to her. Suddenly there was nothing else Amanda would rather do. "Well, there's Memorial Park, but that's so big."

"I'll find you," Kirk said with confidence. "Pick an entrance."

"What about food?"

"I'll take care of it."

Feeling dangerously pleased, Amanda suggested meeting at the southeast entrance and spent the next twenty minutes wondering if her upcoming lunch with Kirk counted as a date.

Then she wondered why it was so important to make the distinction. Couldn't she just relax and enjoy his company?

"WHAT'S THE MATTER?" Kirk popped the lid off a plastic bowl and began attacking the contents with a plastic fork.

Amanda gazed at an identical bowl he'd set in front of her. To her picnics meant hot dogs or sandwiches and warm, squishy fruit, which usually ended up in the garbage. "The men I know don't eat salads."

"This isn't just a *salad*," he said, mixing in some black goop. "This is grilled-chicken-fajita salad with black-bean vinaigrette."

Amanda eyed the little container with the black liquid. "Sounds...trendy."

"Who cares, as long as it tastes good."

If he hadn't been watching her so avidly, she might have picked out the few tortilla chips and eaten those before they got soggy. Reluctantly, she tore off the foil lid and dumped the black dressing on her salad. What a waste of good junk food.

Kirk continued to eat, and Amanda knew she was going to have to taste her salad sooner or later. She picked at a chip.

"If I eat heavy lunches, I'm not sharp in the afternoons. I save the carbs for night." Kirk gestured to the chilled bottle. "Drink your water. People don't drink enough water."

Amanda found herself obediently taking a sip of the designer water. It tasted just like Houston tap water. Under Kirk's watchful eye, she took another sip. What if this foreign water was really plain old tap water? Who'd know the difference? *Bottled waters: The Em-*

*peror's New Clothes?* No. *Bottled waters: Damp Deceit.* Much better. Alliteration always—

"You aren't eating your salad."

To oblige him, Amanda nibbled at a chip.

"That doesn't count."

She made a face and took a big forkful of lettuce, chewed quickly and swallowed. "Hey, that wasn't too bad. It didn't taste as . . . black as I thought."

Kirk chuckled. "You aren't an adventurous eater, I take it."

"I don't give it a lot of thought." Amanda shrugged. "I guess I'm in the habit of grabbing food when I'm hungry. Every time I shop for food, it spoils before I cook it."

"Too tired to cook when you get home?" He set the bowl on the white cloth he'd spread on the ground and unfastened his cuff links.

"I've usually already eaten by then." Amanda watched as Kirk rolled up his shirtsleeves, exposing his arms. "I work crazy hours." She liked the contrast of the white shirt against his skin. Were men's arms supposed to be so attractive?

Kirk retrieved his bowl. "You can get caught up in that trap." He gestured to her salad, prompting her to eat.

Amanda took another bite. The salad didn't taste all that weird. Rather good, in fact. She only hoped her stomach didn't rebel at the unaccustomed fresh greens. "I'd like to point out that you seem caught up in the crazy-work-schedule trap yourself."

"You're right. That's why I consciously schedule in downtime."

"Like picnics?" Amanda plucked at the white cloth.

"Sometimes." He finished his salad and stuffed the bowl into the trash sack. "I borrowed this from our conference room. We frequently have open houses and need a tablecloth."

"But we're getting it dirty!"

"It's washable," he said, unconcerned.

Right. And one of his female brokers would probably take it home to wash. Amanda was coming to realize that they spoiled him.

"Try to relax and enjoy the weather." He leaned back, propping himself on his elbows. "A front is due in this weekend."

Amanda studied him as she ate. He had a lean look, and coupled with this salad stuff and the water, she'd guess he was a fitness buff. He probably ran five miles every morning.

Her fork scraped the bottom of the plastic bowl, and Amanda stared down in surprise. She'd actually finished her salad. "That wasn't bad," she said, handing him the bowl. "You're into this health stuff, huh?"

"Not really." He tossed a foil-wrapped lump toward her. It plopped onto the tablecloth. "I just enjoy good food."

"What's this?" Amanda poked at the top. Too hard for tofu.

"Killer brownies."

"Ooh, they're still warm!" Amanda ripped open the foil and bit into a taste of heaven. "*This* is food."

They didn't say anything for the next few minutes, but it was a comfortable silence, one Amanda hated to break. However... "The reason I called you was to talk about Virginia's Santa reports."

"Isn't that all finished?"

Amanda smoothed the crinkles out of the foil so she could collect the last of the brownie crumbs. "Malls just outside Houston want their Santas rated, too."

"There's only been the one report. How'd the other malls find out about it?"

"We've been advertising. Anyway, I wanted to know if I could drive Virginia out there this week." *Or you could. Then we could have a repeat of Saturday.*

"If it's all right with Virginia, it's all right with me. When were you planning to go?"

Amanda toyed with the idea of suggesting Saturday, but Kay would have a fit if she didn't have the reports in the can. "I'll have to find out when her Christmas pageant rehearsals are scheduled."

Kirk looked blank. "Virginia's in a Christmas pageant? When did that happen?"

Amanda explained. "She has a part in her school's Christmas program. She's really excited. I'm surprised she didn't tell you about it."

"Haven't really seen her all that much since Saturday." At Amanda's accusing look, he explained, "I was at the office most of yesterday and had a breakfast meeting today."

"Hmm." Checking for any stray brownie crumbs, Amanda gave up and wadded the foil. It wasn't her place to criticize Kirk's relationship with his daughter, but a nudge or two in the right direction wouldn't hurt. "I know she'd like to spend more time with you."

A shadow passed over his face. "I'm doing the best I can."

Amanda shouldn't have brought it up. Most single mothers of her acquaintance carried around a heavy load of guilt. It was sexist of her to think that single fathers wouldn't, as well. "I'm sorry."

He waved off her apology. "I only wish I had more time." He regarded her for a moment before adding, "Then I could spend some with *you,* too."

She glanced away. "I thought we were talking about Virginia."

Kirk shifted until he was leaning on one elbow, facing her. "So talk."

Actually, there was nothing more to say, unless Amanda was prepared to lecture him on his daughter. And who was she to lecture on parenting?

"Well?" he prompted at her continued silence.

She looked up. His expression told her that he knew she was using Virginia as a buffer.

"I'd like to see you again," he said with a directness she couldn't ignore. "Do you feel the same way?"

She drew a knee up to her chest. Tucking her hair behind her ear, she gazed at the traffic outside the park and tried to think of a response.

It was a straightforward, we're-too-old-for-games kind of question, and it deserved an answer in kind. Unfortunately Amanda didn't have one. "I don't know."

"Fair enough." The plastic bowls cracked as Kirk crumpled the trash, obviously preparing to leave—obviously interpreting "I don't know" as "no."

Amanda didn't mean "no," and she wasn't ready for their lunch to end. "I don't date much," she felt compelled to say. "I suppose you could say I don't date at all."

His gaze flicked over her. "That's clearly your choice."

Amanda smiled. "Thanks."

Kirk got to his feet and deposited their trash in a green can. When he turned back, the golden autumn sunlight gilded his face and hair, momentarily dazzling her.

*This man is interested in you, the key word being "man." Mature. Successful. Responsible. Considerate. He's not a selfish kid like Trenton was.*

"I was married once," Amanda said all in a rush. "I'm a little skittish about starting...relationships." She wished she hadn't had to use the "r" word.

Kirk stood over her, hands in his pockets. Amanda knew he'd planned to pull up the tablecloth, walk her to her car and bid her farewell. Probably forever.

Or at least until Virginia brought them together again.

She could tell he was still thinking about it by the way he stood there.

"What happened?" he asked at last, easing himself back onto the tablecloth.

"We were both too young." Grasping her knees, Amanda continued, "I quit college to support him while he went to law school. He grew. I didn't." It was as simple as that.

She braced herself for the old feelings of bitterness and was surprised when they didn't come.

"And you've been making up for lost time ever since, right?"

He *was* right. Amanda didn't like knowing that he'd analyzed her so easily. "Dipping into the pop-psychology books?"

"Regular psychology books, actually," he corrected without taking offense. "I'm selling homes, not just houses. If I can figure out what a family wants—not just what they say they want, but what's really important to them—I've got a better chance of making a sale."

"What kind of a house would you show me?"

Kirk sat up and brushed at his slacks. "You aren't the house type. I'd steer you toward a small apartment in an exclusive high rise with a health club on the top floor—"

"I'd never use it."

"No, but you'd feel healthier knowing it was there if you ever changed your mind."

He was good, Amanda thought. "What else?"

"There'd have to be a doorman and maid service, a restaurant next door, and ideally this would all be located right by your studio."

"Perfect. Where do I sign?"

Kirk grinned and hooked a thumb over his shoulder. "Other than Briar Oaks over there, Houston isn't much for high-rise apartment buildings."

"I knew it sounded too good to be true." Amanda sighed. "Probably out of my price range, anyway."

Kirk regarded her for a moment. "Not for long. You look like you're a woman on the move."

His observation pleased her, because that's what she wanted to be. Reluctantly looking at her watch, Amanda stood. "And I'd better be moving on back to the studio." She shook out the tablecloth, roughly folding it.

"You never answered my question." Kirk took the bundle from her. "Shall we get together again?"

Amanda didn't want to answer that question. She had a nice life and a goal. There wasn't enough room for a man with Kirk's responsibilities. Would it be fair to start something that couldn't go anywhere? Did she want to put herself through that?

And it wasn't just Kirk. There was Virginia to consider, too. Kids didn't understand about grown-ups and goals.

The breeze pulled her hair across her face. Before Amanda could tuck it back behind her ear, Kirk reached out and did it for her.

He trailed his fingers along the length of her jaw, his thumb moving in a light caress.

Amanda inhaled softly. He was reminding her of their kiss. He was thinking about it, too. She could tell by the softened but still intense look in his eyes.

Then his lips were on hers, and she didn't need reminding anymore. She didn't need to think about her decision anymore, either.

"Well?" he whispered, his mouth teasing the corner of hers.

"Yes," she heard herself answer, and laughed. "Definitely yes."

# CHAPTER EIGHT

THE WEEK FLEW BY and Amanda was almost too busy to notice that Kirk hadn't called her. Almost.

"Daddy says hi," Virginia reported on one of their drives to yet another mall. She never seemed bored by their trips, or visiting Santa Claus after Santa Claus. When they returned to the studio to tape the rating segments, Virginia remembered where to stand and what to say. She could have a career in this business, if she wanted to, Amanda thought.

"Tell *Daddy* hi back," Amanda replied, wondering why Daddy didn't say hi himself.

She wasn't going to call first. Absolutely not. If it was meant to be, then it would happen. Her life was fine just the way it was. She had stories to produce. Promotions to get. She even had a five-foot-long sleep pillow that was just fine to hug at night. And it didn't snore.

There was no way she'd call first.

She sat in her cubicle and stared at the telephone. Come to think of it, no one had called her in a while. Maybe the phone was broken, she thought, reaching for it.

"Amanda!" Kay stuck her head into the cubicle.

Amanda snatched her hand from the phone.

"What's the kid's schedule?"

Amanda didn't need to ask who "the kid" was. Virginia was becoming a celebrity. The ratings for the after-school portion of the program were up.

But that paled beside the fact that their nightly newscast had, for the first time ever, actually beaten one of the network affiliates in that time slot.

There was great rejoicing at the "Hello Houston" studios.

This morning a talent agent had contacted them, wanting to know if Virginia was being represented. Amanda tried to tell him there was nothing to represent, but he wouldn't believe her.

She probably ought to tell Kirk about that. Who knows? Maybe Virginia could act in a television commercial or two. It was a great way to build up a college fund.

Amanda would remember to mention it when Kirk phoned.

"Amanda? Hello?" Still in the doorway, Kay waved her hand back and forth.

"Sorry. I was thinking."

"Look." Kay walked into Amanda's office and thrust a pile of pink message slips at her. "All calls about the kid."

"Yes, the public likes her."

Kay glanced around the clutter in the office, then shoved aside a pile of phone books on the desk and sat perilously close to Amanda's leftover coffee.

"These aren't from the public." Kay put on her reading glasses and thumbed through the papers. "Malls and wannabe Santa Clauses. Radio stations—one of them is considering holding a Santa Claus contest, and they want Virginia to judge."

"Oh, for heaven's sake." With everything going on in the world, *this* was what excited the masses?

"What's on your docket?" Kay asked, and turned around Amanda's desk calendar.

"Just finishing up a few stories."

"Hmm." Kay flipped through the calendar pages.

"Then I'll start my child-safety piece," Amanda said pointedly.

"The Santa reports come first," her boss decreed. "Clear away everything. If you need help, ask. Maria Alvarez—"

"No!"

Kay stared at her over the tops of her glasses.

"I can handle everything." That was all Amanda needed—Maria Alvarez being assigned the child-safety story.

Kay opened her mouth, probably to do that very thing, when the telephone rang.

Amanda snatched it up in midring. "It's for you," she said, ungraciously thrusting the handset at Kay.

Kay listened silently, but her eyes grew wide. "When?" she asked sharply, and motioned for a pencil and paper. "How big?"

Amanda's foot twitched. A breaking story! And Kay was in her office. Finally, some luck.

"*How* many people?" Kay stopped writing.

A disaster. It had to be a disaster. Something probably exploded. No, a hostage situation. Someone crazed by too many repetitions of "Jingle Bells" had gone berserk—

"Amanda!" Kay slammed down the phone and scribbled on the notepad.

"What do you need?" Amanda concentrated on sounding calm and competent. Talk about being in the right place at the right time. Did that guy over in news still have access to an extra bullet-proof vest?

"Can you go to Dallas this weekend?"

A field assignment. This was *great*. "Yes. What's the story?"

"KDAL has engineered a media event. Since Virginia can't find the real Santa in Houston, they want her to go rate the Santas in Dallas."

"AND SO THEY WANT HER to go rate the Santas in Dallas." Amanda tried to inject enthusiasm into her recital.

Kirk ran his fingers through his hair, something he rarely did, and stared at the house in front of him. "Hasn't this whole thing gotten out of hand?"

Amanda certainly thought so, but didn't dare say. "You never know what's going to hit the public's fancy. Virginia and her candy-cane ratings just touch people." People with too much time at their disposal.

Kirk sighed and checked his watch. He and Amanda were leaning against his car, which was parked in front of a rambling house on a wooded lot in the silk-stocking Memorial area. "Look, I've got a couple coming to view this house in a minute. I—" He broke off and shoved his hands into his pockets.

If Amanda hadn't known better, she'd have sworn he was nervous. Glancing at the house, she figured he had a right to be. It was an architect's nightmare. No, it was several architects' nightmare. Amanda knew next to nothing about houses, but even she could see that this one sprawled across the lot like a crazy quilt of architectural styles.

"I don't know." Kirk sighed again. "I don't know if it's a good thing for Virginia to go to Dallas."

This wasn't the same Kirk who'd brought her on a picnic lunch. He was preoccupied, and Amanda probably shouldn't be bothering him when he was working. But she needed an answer, and Rosalie, the receptionist, had told her she didn't expect him back in the office that day.

He wasn't glad to see Amanda. He'd tried to fake it, but not convincingly. After a moment or two, he'd stopped trying.

Unfortunately Kirk wasn't the only one who was working. Amanda needed an answer now. "It might not have occurred to you, but Virginia could use this opportunity to her advantage. I had a talent agent call me this morning."

"What?" He'd been staring down the street. Now she had his full attention.

"A talent agent. If Virginia wanted to, she could probably make a few commercials, or more if you decided to push it."

"Why would I want to push it?"

"I don't know—college money?"

Kirk gave her a forbidding look. "I can pay for her college."

"I didn't mean to imply that you couldn't." Amanda jammed her hand into her pocket and began rubbing the worry stone. "Just that *if* you ever thought about an acting career for Virginia, she's in a good negotiating position right now."

"Don't be absurd." Kirk pulled back his cuff to inspect his watch again.

"Listen, I've got to get back to my producer. She needs to call that radio station."

Instead of answering, Kirk drummed his fingers on the hood of his car and stared at the end of the block.

Amanda stepped into his line of sight. "What about Dallas this weekend?"

"Amanda—" he met her eyes fully for the first time since she'd arrived "—I don't think so. We've got to call a halt to this sometime."

"How about sometime later?"

His gaze flicked away as he shook his head slightly.

"Christmas Eve is in three weeks. It'll end then, for certain. Frankly, Virginia's having a good time. Remember Saturday?"

A corner of his mouth tilted upward. "Yes."

"So?" She smiled brightly. "Let's do it again in Dallas."

He considered for a moment, then shook his head once more.

Amanda hadn't expected opposition. She'd been looking forward to a repeat of that Saturday. Obviously Kirk hadn't.

Okay. She got the message. Something had happened since their picnic and he wanted to blow off their fledgling relationship. Fine. Well, not fine, but she'd explore that later. In the meantime, whatever might have been between them shouldn't affect Virginia's reports.

"Oh, come on." She put a hand on his arm. "They promised to drive us around in a limousine. Virginia will just—"

Kirk pulled his arm away. "I said *no!*"

Amanda was shocked into silence.

"I don't want to think about Dallas. I don't have time to go to Dallas. I'm trying to sell a house here!"

Amanda, her mouth working, backed away. She tripped down the curb, her arms flailing as she tried to regain her balance.

Kirk grabbed her before she fell, hauling her into his arms. "I'm sorry, I'm sorry," he repeated again and again, holding her close.

Amanda clung to him, even when she'd regained her balance. No one had held her like this in a long time. She could hear his heart thumping against her ear and for a moment surrendered to the desire to feel cherished.

"It's this house." Kirk drew a ragged breath. "It's this damn house."

She heard the pain in his voice and forced herself to lift her head. He probably regretted his show of emotion. "Hard to sell?" But Amanda knew it was more than that. Kirk was the type of man who'd enjoy the challenge of a tough sell.

He loosened his grip, and she reluctantly pulled away. "The Rambling Ranch is a legend in Houston real-estate circles. It's been for sale off and on for years. The original owners died and the heirs want out from under it."

"I can see why." Amanda turned and leaned against Kirk's car, hoping the two tears that had leaked out the corner of her eyes had evaporated now. Hoped she'd left no wet spots on his tie.

"There's a bonus that members of the board of realtors funded for the person who finally sells this house. Every brand-new agent takes a crack at showing this house."

His voice sounded normal again. Amanda risked a glance at him. "You aren't interested in the money, are you? You just want the distinction of being the person to sell this house."

"I used to. Now it's...personal."

She waited, but he didn't continue. Did he really think she'd abandon the topic after a statement like that? "So what's the story?"

"This is where I met Michelle."

"Virginia's mother." Now Amanda understood his edginess.

"Yeah." He still stared down to the end of the block, but Amanda realized he wasn't seeing the trees or watching for cars. He was remembering his wife. "We were both hotshot brokers determined to sell this house. One day, we showed up here at the same time. I had an artsy-type couple and she was dragging along some rich foreigner."

Amanda laughed. "Did she think foreigners have no taste?"

Kirk grinned. "I believe her reasoning was that he was so rich she could sell him on the merits of the location, with the idea that he'd tear down the house."

"What happened?"

"A military coup, I think. He went back to his own country."

"And your artsy couple?"

"Wanted to live in a different area of town."

*And Michelle?* While Amanda was deciding whether she really wanted to hear about Kirk's wife—since he obviously still mourned her and since he just as obviously had changed his mind about a possible relationship—he continued talking.

"Three months after that, we were married."

"That was quick."

Kirk shrugged. "I knew what I wanted and so did she. No need to waste time."

*Unlike me,* Amanda thought. *I've wasted a lot of time.*

"She was my partner in McEnery Realtors." He shook his head. "Talk about struggling. We picked the absolute worst time in Houston real-estate history to start an agency. We didn't care, though. We were going to sell this house and the commission would carry us for months.''

''But you didn't sell the house.''

''No one else did, either.'' His mouth tightened and he drew a quick, hard breath. ''She . . . was on her way over here to show it when she died.''

The revelation was so unexpected that Amanda gasped, involuntarily clutching his arm. Kirk had turned and leaned both arms over the roof of the car.

''An auto accident?'' Amanda whispered.

He shook his head no. ''A brain aneurysm. Her car just kept going and hit the brick wall that lines Memorial Drive.''

''How horrible. When . . . ?''

''. . . did it happen?'' he completed the question for her. ''Almost four years ago. I met her, married her, became a father and lost her all in seven months.''

As Amanda searched for something to say, Kirk nodded toward the end of the street. ''They're here.''

''I'll leave you.'' Amanda quickly walked to her car and opened the door.

''Amanda?'' Kirk called to her, but watched the approach of the other car. ''About Dallas . . .''

As he hesitated, Amanda held her breath.

''I'll be tied up here. But if you want to take Virginia, and she wants to go, then it's okay.''

*Yippee.* ''Thanks,'' Amanda said, and hopped in her car before he could change his mind. Or before she could change hers.

''I WANT TO GO fill up the ice bucket,'' Virginia announced.

Amanda was already stretched across the bed, her eyes closed. ''Do you know where the ice machine is?''

There was a telling hesitation before a confident, "Uh-huh."

*Liar,* Amanda thought without anger. She was tired. Why wasn't Virginia tired? And when did a puddle-jumper flight like Houston to Dallas become such an ordeal? How many packets of peanuts had Virginia eaten in the hour, anyway?

"Wait a minute and I'll go with you."

Virginia frowned.

"I want to stretch my legs." Okay, so now Amanda was a liar, too.

"You don't trust me," Virginia accused her.

With a supreme effort of will, Amanda dragged herself off the bed. "I trust you, kiddo, but there are some weirdos in this world I don't."

"Will they be at the ice machine?" A hopeful smile crept across her features.

"Knowing my luck," Amanda grumbled, unlocking the door. She wore no shoes. They seemed tight and confining after her first experience traveling with a child since she'd *been* a child.

Virginia ran down the hall, checking corridors for the ice machine. Then she reported on her findings to Amanda. Amanda had no problem with Virginia running—that used up energy—but she seemed unable to communicate except by shouting.

She'd found the ice machine and was filling the bucket by using her hands, instead of the metal scoop, when Amanda caught up with her.

"What can I have to drink?" Virginia asked as Amanda handed her the scoop.

A quick glance told Amanda that all the drinks for sale contained caffeine. No way. "It's too late for a drink." Except a giant double-strength margarita. "Gosh, it's almost time for bed." Amanda didn't have to fake the yawn that followed. "I'll buy you a drink in the morning."

"What time is it?" Virginia grabbed Amanda's wrist. "Eight thirty-two," she said, disgusted. "Only babies go to bed this early."

"Babies and associate producers," Amanda corrected.

"I'll go to bed after Daddy gets here," Virginia announced, putting the lid back on the ice bucket.

Amanda studied her warily. Hadn't Kirk told Virginia he wasn't coming to Dallas? Or had that rat left it to Amanda to break the bad news?

"Can I have a drink now?"

"Uh . . . I didn't bring my purse."

"Well, go *get* it."

Amanda took a step backward and crunched a piece of ice. "Ow!" The sound reverberated around the tiny uncarpeted room.

"Shh!" Virginia said.

Limping wetly back to their room, Amanda scoured her mind for a way to let the little girl know that her daddy wasn't coming.

"When's Daddy coming?" Virginia bounced on Amanda's bed and crawled over to her purse.

Amanda took it and quickly counted the change. There'd been a snack machine, too. Maybe Virginia could be bought off with potato chips.

"When's . . . Daddy . . . coming?" Virginia repeated, punctuating each word with a bounce.

"You'll see him when you get home on Sunday. Here's a dollar in quarters, and I've got nickels and dimes, too. Want something to eat?" Amanda smiled gamely and extended a handful of change.

"I want to see him now." Virginia accepted the money and slid off the bed.

"Your dad's back in Houston." Amanda ran to open the door. "Remember the airplane trip?" Amanda knew *she* wouldn't soon forget it. "We're in Dallas. Dallas is a long way from Houston." Wrong thing to say. "I don't mean *long* long," she backpedaled. "But we'd have to drive several hours in the car, which is why we flew in the airplane."

Virginia's eyes were wide. A dime rolled to the floor.

"C'mon. Let's go find something to eat." Amanda smiled as if everything was just fine, hoping that it would be.

It wasn't.

"I want my Daddy." Virginia's eyes were bright with tears and her nose had turned pink.

"You'll see your daddy before you know it. We'll have our snack and put on our jammies and sleep. Then tomorrow we'll visit lots of Santa Clauses and sleep some more." Amanda spoke faster and faster, racing Virginia's impending tears. "We'll fly on another airplane, and when you get home, your daddy will be there." And he better be, too.

"I want to go *home!*"

"You will. Right now, we're...we're having an adventure. Just you and me. On a road trip." Amanda stood by the open door, grinning inanely. "And we're just about to eat a lot of junk food, and there's nobody to stop us!"

Virginia ran out the door, but she didn't go in the direction of the snack machines.

"Virginia!" Amanda caught up with her at the elevator. "The machines are down that way."

"I want to go home. You can't make me stay!" Virginia's voice was shrill.

"Virginia…" Amanda took her arm just as a man and woman exited the elevator.

"No!" Virginia shrieked. "I want my Daddy! I don't want to stay with you!" She beat on Amanda's arm.

The couple stared.

"Shh!" Amanda sent an embarrassed smile to the couple.

They didn't smile back.

"Her father is in Houston," Amanda explained, knowing the couple thought the worst.

Wailing, Virginia sagged to the floor, forcing Amanda to let go or fall over herself. "I want Da-a-addy!"

The couple didn't move and the man took a step toward Virginia. Amanda was conscious that at least one hotel room door had opened and the occupant had come out to stare at them.

"Virginia … *Virginia!*" Amanda had to shout. She'd never felt so helpless in her life. "Let's go call your dad. Wouldn't you like to talk to your daddy?"

Sobbing, Virginia nodded and stood up.

Weak with relief, Amanda hustled her back down the hall and into their room. She grabbed the phone. "Okay, what's your home number?" Amanda had it in her purse, but hoped to distract the crying child.

*Kirk McEnery, you'd better be home.*

He was. As soon as Amanda heard his voice, she thrust the telephone at Virginia, not even speaking to Kirk.

"Daddy!" Virginia wailed.

A tense Amanda sat on the opposite bed and waited.

Five minutes passed. Then ten. Over and over Virginia asked for him to come or insisted on going home.

Why hadn't Kirk told her he wasn't coming with them?

After fifteen minutes, Amanda wondered why she didn't have a throbbing headache. She was certainly entitled.

"Okay." Virginia handed the telephone to Amanda.

This was one call she didn't want to take.

"Hello?" she warbled, trying to bluff her way through this.

"*What* have you done to her?"

"Nothing," Amanda replied, not liking his accusing tone.

"She's hysterical."

"*Yes, I know.*" Amanda's voice made it clear that she was well aware of Virginia's hysteria and had been for some time.

She heard him sigh. "I should've never let you take her up there."

"That's what I thought you'd say."

"Can you blame me?"

Amanda had strong opinions on that subject, but knew better than to voice them.

"Is he coming?" Virginia whispered.

Kirk must have heard her. "Tell her I'm coming and that she'd better get her little rear in bed right now!"

"SHE'S ASLEEP," Amanda whispered.

It was well after midnight when a weary Kirk tapped on the room door. He pushed past Amanda, strode to the bed and stared down at his daughter.

Naturally she looked like an angel. No resemblance at all to the shrieking child Amanda had been forced to deal with earlier.

Shooting Amanda a dark look, Kirk beckoned for her to follow him out into the hall.

Amanda slipped the room key into her vest pocket and pulled the door shut behind her. Then she leaned against it, bracing herself for his blast of anger.

"What happened?" Although the overriding emotion in his voice was concern, Amanda heard the anger simmering beneath it.

"Virginia seemed to think you were going to meet us here."

Kirk's eyes narrowed. "Who gave her that idea?"

"Well, *I* didn't!"

He thrust his hands into the pockets of his leather bomber jacket, his expression remote. "Mrs. Webster and I explained the trip to her. This morning, when I said goodbye, I went through the usual 'behave yourself' routine and told her I'd see her on Sunday."

"Well, somehow, she got the idea that you'd be here with us."

"*Somehow?*"

Amanda didn't like the way he said that. "Are you accusing me of manipulating Virginia so you'd fly up here?" They might as well get it out into the open.

"Yes," he replied without hesitation.

She wanted blunt, she got blunt. "Why would I do that?"

He made a derisive sound. "For the same reason every woman feels she has to exercise her maternal prowess and interfere in my relationship with Virginia."

"I *have* no maternal prowess! Three hours with me and she's hysterical."

"So you need a little practice."

She straightened, suddenly feeling uncomfortably close to him, but Kirk didn't move back. "For your much-needed edification," she declared, not giving ground even though she was near enough to feel the heat of his body, "I don't want any practice."

"You don't see yourself as a mother?"

Amanda shook her head. "And this trip confirms it."

Some of the anger left his face as he realized she was serious. "Being a parent isn't all bad." He half smiled. "If I can do it, anybody can."

"Being a parent is time-consuming, a lot of trouble and a lot of hassle." She drew a deep breath. "And it's not for me."

She swallowed, knowing she'd just killed any hope of a romance with Kirk McEnery—as if their argument hadn't already.

He must have known it, too. "You're basing your whole impression of parenthood on one difficult evening?" His mouth twisted. "I hope you're more diligent in researching your television programs."

Amanda bristled. Criticizing her mothering abilities was one thing; attacking her professionalism was out of line. "You forget, I've spent a *lot* of time with Virginia lately—probably more than you."

Her rebuke hit home. "I do have a business to run," he reminded her, his voice cold.

"Yes, you have a time-consuming job with erratic hours." She pressed her palm against her chest. "*I* have a time-consuming job with erratic hours. Frankly, *neither* of us has time for a child." Amanda gasped. She hadn't meant to say the last part out loud.

Kirk's face whitened in outrage. "Virginia and I are managing just fine!"

"That's because all those women you accused of *interfering* are taking care of Virginia for you."

"That's not true."

And Amanda could tell he honestly believed it. Even she, with no parenting experience at all, could see that he was headed for trouble with Virginia. It was a classic case. Virginia had thrown an old-fashioned tantrum this evening to get attention from her father—and it had worked. Amanda knew Virginia's ploys had worked in the past and would probably work in the future. Kirk seemed completely unaware.

But it was late and she was tired and angry. This was not the time to be discussing child-rearing—especially when Kirk's relationship with Virginia was none of her business. Once it might have become her business, but she'd pretty well scotched that, so why not warn Kirk that he and his daughter were headed for trouble?

"Not true? Say you're running behind schedule. No problem, someone from your office will pick Virginia up from day care. You have to work late? Virginia waits in your reception area."

"Sometimes that can't be helped."

"I think it happens a lot more than sometimes. You have a whole support system in place, and yet you don't acknowledge how much you depend on it."

As Kirk stared at her, Amanda watched the pain seep into his expression. "Virginia doesn't have two parents—only me. And I have to support us. Anyone in my situation would depend on others some of the time."

"You depend on others *all* of the time," she said as gently as she could. "You have a housekeeper who apparently does everything from making Virginia's medical appointments to shopping for her clothes."

"That's her job."

"That's right—her *job*. You're Virginia's father. When do *you* spend time with her?"

"So I was right." His jaw hardened. "You think I've been neglecting Virginia, so you engineered this little bonding excursion."

Amanda sighed. "I didn't."

"The question is, who was supposed to bond?" He leaned forward, withdrawing a hand from his pocket and placing it on the wall beside her. Amanda felt the doorknob in her back. "Virginia and I, or you and I?"

And she'd actually once, briefly, been *attracted* to him.

"You egotistical jerk!" She raised her hand to push him back, and he caught her wrist.

"I told you I wanted to see you again. And you told me you needed time to think. So I gave you time." Amanda pulled, but he didn't let go. "What happened? Did you panic and think I'd lost interest?"

"You think I'm so desperate for a man that I'd take advantage of a child?" She wrenched her wrist away. "I'm not desperate. I don't *need* a man. And I don't need you."

She tried to push past him so that he'd go away and she could escape into the hotel room.

He didn't give an inch.

Amanda refused to, either.

They stared at each other, breathing heavily, chests rising and falling. Then Kirk grabbed Amanda and pulled her to him, kissing her hard.

And Amanda, to her utter astonishment, kissed him back.

In a corner of her mind, she wondered why she was kissing him. In the movies, whenever the hero grabbed the heroine and kissed her during an argument, Amanda had always hoped the heroine would kick the guy in the shins. Of course, the heroine rarely did. She always put up a feeble protest with a few light thumps on the shoulders.

Amanda tried thumping herself—after a betraying hesitation. She balled her fists and pounded Kirk's leather-clad shoulders ineffectively. Ineffectively, because she couldn't get much leverage. Ineffectively, because she was afraid he'd stop.

Besides, she'd discovered what those movie heroines must have discovered—that the contact of fists against muscled shoulders just emphasized the hero's masculine strength. And every feminine atom in Amanda's being was currently responding to that masculine strength.

Kirk, like a classic movie hero, had bent her backward, forcing her to cling to him or lose her balance and fall against the doorknob. And Amanda, just like an outdated celluloid heroine, curled her fingers over Kirk's shoulders, wrapped her arms around him and kissed him for all she was worth.

During an argument, hearts pounded and emotions were high. Starting a kiss when emotions were already heightened led to an almost immediate explosion. *That's* what those wimpy but sly heroines had figured out.

Smart girls, Amanda thought as she and Kirk tried to melt into one another.

# CHAPTER NINE

AMANDA HAD NO IDEA how long she and Kirk kissed in the hallway outside her hotel room, but it was long enough for her to doubt all her goals and ideas about herself. Ever since the breakup of her marriage, she'd decided to abandon domesticity. Not for her the life of diapers, car pools, PTA and yard-of-the-month.

She was determined to be a full producer—soon. And then she was going after Kay's job. If Kay hadn't moved on or up, then Amanda was fully prepared to leave "Hello Houston." She wanted to remain mobile. Rootless.

Kirk was an incompatible complication, no matter that his every kiss screamed compatibility.

"You do care," he whispered.

"Yes," she murmured. She cared. Deeply.

"I was too angry to understand." His gaze caressed her face, then he held her close, his chin resting on the top of her head. "I guess I haven't been as good a father as I thought."

Amanda felt awful. "Virginia adores you. She only wants to be with you more. You're all she's got."

Kirk held Amanda away until he could look into her eyes. "Maybe that can change."

His expression had a questioning vulnerability that made Amanda want to fling her arms around him and commit herself wholeheartedly. But she held back. It was too soon.

"It's getting late," she said, and stood on tiptoe to press her lips briefly against his.

He gave her an infinitesimal nod. "See you in the morning."

For hours after Amanda and Kirk had said their goodnights, she lay in her bed and, accompanied by Virginia's even breathing, reexamined the choices she'd made for her life.

The self-examination continued the next morning while Amanda helped Virginia get ready. What would it be like to do this every morning? It wasn't so bad. Virginia could dress herself and only needed help positioning the huge Christmas bow in her hair.

When Amanda caught herself mentally rearranging her own morning schedule, she stopped and took a deep breath.

What had happened to her? she wondered, but already knew the answer. Virginia and Kirk had happened to her, that was what.

Down in the lobby, Amanda watched Virginia launch herself at her father with a squeal of delight.

Kirk hugged her, then leaned over and kissed a surprised Amanda on the cheek. "Good morning." His voice was low and intimate, leaving Amanda in no doubt of his feelings.

It was her own feelings she doubted. "Good morning," she echoed automatically, her gaze darting to Virginia. What did she think of her father's kiss?

Virginia's big blue eyes shifted from one adult to the other. And then she smiled.

They moved to the restaurant and sat, the very picture of a happy family. The scent of Kirk's shaving cream lingered faintly, and the feel of his freshly shaven cheek had triggered memories of familial intimacy.

"What's that say, Daddy?" Virginia pointed to the words under the illustrations on the children's menu.

"I thought you were supposed to be learning how to read," Kirk said.

"But it's hard and I'm *hungry!*" Virginia protested, her face beginning to crumple into an ominously familiar expression.

"Why don't you help her sound out the words?" Amanda suggested.

Kirk shot her a look, then spread open the menu and pointed to a picture of two eggs and bacon made into a happy face.

Sighing, Virginia began testing her fledgling reading skills.

Amanda released the breath she'd been holding. She'd been a bit too heavy-handed.

Virginia decided on French toast with scrambled eggs, gave her order to the waitress and beamed at her father and Amanda. "I wish we could do this every morning."

"Eat out?" Kirk asked.

Virginia shook her head. "Eat with Amanda." She grinned and added slyly, "Wouldn't that be great?"

Amanda glanced from the gapped-tooth grin to Kirk. He regarded her with a challenging smile. "Yes, it would."

Thoroughly rattled, Amanda added too much sugar to her coffee and then burned her tongue.

After breakfast, a limousine sent by KDAL arrived to ferry them from mall to mall. No sneak Santa visits, these.

At the first mall, local radio and television personalities awaited Virginia. Blond elves with big Texas hair

whisked her to the head of the line and ignored Amanda's feeble protests about grading the waiting time to see
Santa, which Virginia had added to her reports ever since
the incident at Buffalo Bayou Mall in Houston.

She discovered her own "Hello Houston" crew jock-
eying for position among Dallas-area television camera
crews. Squeezing next to Ron, she asked, "Are you here
for the entire day?"

"No." he shifted the camera on his shoulder. "We've
got a noon flight back."

Shaking her head, Amanda retreated. This whole
Santa thing was way over budget, and she hoped she
wouldn't be held responsible.

"What a circus," she grumbled to Kirk as a high
school choral group serenaded Virginia while she sat on
Santa's lap.

"No, it's just Christmas," he replied with an amused
smile.

"Same thing."

A light in the glittery white tree branches near them
blinked annoyingly. Kirk idly tapped it with his finger,
then pushed the bulb farther into its socket. "What do
you have against Christmas?"

"Nothing," Amanda lied, as she'd been lying to herself for years.

"Mmm." The little light beamed steadily. Kirk gave a
satisfied nod. "Since you won't tell me, I'll take a guess."
He tilted his head and studied her.

Amanda met his eyes, until his perceptive gaze made
her look away.

"Someone hurt you at Christmastime."

Amanda refused to answer, instead brushing white
glitter off her black pants. So he'd made a lucky guess.

"Am I right?" he pursued with a determination that let her know he wasn't going to quit until he knew everything.

"Yes!" Amanda snapped, crossing her arms over her chest. "My marriage broke up, okay?" She turned her head and concentrated on the Christmas-card-like tableau in front of her.

"I'm sorry," Kirk said quietly. "But you can't blame your marital troubles on Christmas."

"If it hadn't been Christmas..." She didn't finish.

"You wouldn't have known your marriage was in trouble?" he concluded.

Stiffly, Amanda nodded.

"But you would've known eventually."

Why did he keep prying? But she knew why. After last night's kisses, after he'd told her all about the weird house in Memorial, he wanted to know about her marriage. If only the whole mess weren't so humiliating.

"I hate to see you deny yourself all the joy of the season—"

"What are you—Santa's public-relations elf?"

He didn't get angry the way she thought he would. "You like being cynical, don't you?"

Amanda couldn't meet his gaze. "No." With her foot she brushed fallen glitter toward the base of the tree.

"So what was it? A fight over the presents?"

Amanda squeezed her eyes closed as if she could squeeze out the memories, too. Kirk was so close to the truth she felt sick to her stomach, the same sick she'd felt when she'd discovered Trenton's betrayal. And all the Christmas sights and sounds and smells were bringing back the searing hurt, just as they always did.

"Amanda? Are you all right? No, you're not," Kirk answered his own question. "Come with me." He took her elbow, but Amanda jerked it away.

"I'm *fine.*"

"Nope. Your face is white." Kirk steered her away from the Santa scene to a nearby bench.

"I'm fine," she insisted, but sat, anyway.

They faced Santa's house, with Kirk keeping a parental eye on his daughter. Virginia, bathed in bright lights and surrounded by cameras, chatted with Santa.

"I'm sorry," Kirk said, filling the awkward silence. "I'd assumed that your marriage broke up in the distant past."

"It did." Sighing, Amanda leaned her head against the back of the bench. "But I can't get over the bitterness. It's been nine years, yet every Christmas, I live it all over again."

"Are you still in love with him?"

"Trenton?" She shot him a look of incredulity. "Hardly."

The grim lines around his mouth eased, and he settled back on the bench. "Just wondered."

"Wonder no more."

"Does that mean you're going to tell me what happened?"

Amanda hesitated. "I was trying to avoid it. The whole sordid story makes me look stupid and naive." But maybe telling him would help her avoid her annual bout of self-recrimination.

"It's possible that after nine years of beating yourself up over whatever happened, your memories are distorted."

Not those memories. She could remember every thought, every feeling, every lie. "I found a receipt for an expensive ladies' watch, which I naturally assumed was Trenton's Christmas present to me. The amount was so much more than I'd spent on him that I felt guilty and full of love." Amanda spoke in a self-deriding, singsong voice.

"How old were you?" Kirk interrupted.

Amanda shrugged. "Twenty . . . twenty-one."

"You were young."

"But old enough to know better."

"Oh, lighten up on yourself."

Amanda smiled wryly, realizing he was trying to make her feel better. "I was already working two jobs or I would have taken on another just to buy him a better present."

"And where was Trenton working?"

"Trenton was still in law school full-time."

"Ah."

Amanda winced. There it was—that knowing expression people got when they thought they could fill in the rest of the story. The horrible thing was, they could. It had happened to student marriages before and would happen again. Amanda had just never thought it would happen to her.

"Go on," he urged.

"You know the rest." Amanda took a deep breath and started to stand.

Kyle put a hand over hers. "Tell me."

She hadn't wanted to, but his gentle command breached her defenses. She'd never told a single person the entire story all at once.

Kirk laced his fingers through hers. Amanda felt the warmth and the unspoken support.

"I . . . I bought him a watch, too," she began. "I thought it was terribly romantic and kind of Frank Capra-ish. You know, exhausted wife on the way to work, passing the jewelry store, desperately saving enough for the watch in the window—hoping she could buy it before someone else did.'' She slid a glance toward him. ''Just imagine every sentimental Christmas movie you've ever seen and you'll get the idea.''

Kirk brushed a flake of plastic snow from her sleeve. ''At the risk of adding to your cliché collection, don't be so hard on yourself.''

''I've already got that one in my collection.''

He chuckled. ''So what happened? Didn't he like the watch?''

''Oh, he loved it. Felt it was just the thing for a lawyer. Had the gall to admire it and thank me—he put on a good show.''

''And *your* watch?''

Amanda swallowed. ''All Christmas day I waited, thinking any moment he'd surprise me with my present.''

''Stop.'' He winced. ''I can't stand holiday pathos.''

''I warned you.'' She was telling her awful story and he was making fun. Unfortunately it did sound like the plot to a B movie and not the terrible tragedy she'd made it out to be all these years.

''And how does this tale of woe end?''

This was the part that usually made Amanda want to bury her head under her pillow. ''I thought he'd realized that we couldn't afford such an expensive gift and had taken it back, so I called the jewelry store just before New Year's. They told me he'd picked up the watch and that it'd been engraved. 'Until it's our time,' or something equally corny.''

Kirk's lips quivered. After a shocked moment when she thought he was laughing *at* her, Amanda started to laugh, too. For the first time the pain wasn't as sharp.

"Isn't that awful?" Her smile faded. "He'd been having an affair and the watch was for *her*."

"Now that's pathos," he said with sympathetic amusement. "But why have you been blaming yourself? It's obvious you were the wronged party."

"Because, even after I talked with the jeweler, I *still* didn't figure it out." Amanda gripped the edge of the wooden bench so hard her fingernails marred the wood. "I had no idea he was seeing anyone else. I thought he was studying."

"You were working two jobs. How could you have known?"

"If I'd been a better wife—"

"Amanda, don't."

The quietly worded command calmed her. Shuddering, she drew a breath and swallowed, releasing her grip on the bench. "I obsessed over that watch," she continued, in control once again. "We weren't having an anniversary and it wasn't my birthday. I couldn't stand not knowing, so guess what I did?"

"Tore up your apartment looking for it?"

"After that."

Kirk laughed, but shook his head.

"I broke my perfectly good watch to give him an excuse to present me with the new one." Amanda looked down at the watch she wore now, the one she'd bought for herself. Later. "When he didn't, I confessed I knew all about the watch he'd bought and he'd better give it to me now or I'd think he'd bought it for another woman."

"And he had." Kirk put his arm around her.

Grateful, Amanda leaned toward him. "I'll never forget his face—frozen. Waiting. Waiting for me to realize that there *was* another woman. A fellow law intern. He hadn't wanted to hurt me, he said, so he was going to wait until after graduation to tell me—coincidentally allowing me to support him for six more months." Even now, embarrassment at the thought of how gullible she'd been made her cheeks burn.

"Amanda, he was a jerk and he used you."

"But why couldn't I tell he was that kind of person? I was left with nothing. Less than nothing—all the debts were in my name since I was the only one employed." She hugged herself. "He'd paid for that watch with cash advances on my credit card, then *I* had to make the payments so my credit rating wouldn't go bad."

"And so you hate Christmas."

"I have good reason." She looked away and noticed that the choir had finished caroling Virginia and that the little girl was being interviewed. She still sat on Santa's lap. Amanda nudged Kirk and pointed. Nodding, he indicated that they should return to the Santa scene.

He was silent as they walked, then said thoughtfully, "You need some different Christmas memories."

Amanda thought she had all the Christmas memories she could stand.

"At the risk of sounding preachy, you could help a family down on their luck. You could volunteer at a soup kitchen, visit a hospital, decorate a nursing home. Something to make a difference."

His words caused a guilty twinge, but she ignored it. "A bunch of colored lights and shiny tinsel isn't going to erase the world's problems."

"So cynical." He stopped walking and Amanda glanced back at him. "I was right before—you *do* enjoy being cynical."

"I do not!" she denied. A woman wearing headphones shushed her.

"Yes, you do, because then you feel superior to the rest of us." Kirk crossed his arms, a challenge in his smile.

"Look at this." Her arm panned the area. "People expect miracles at Christmas—do they think they can find them at a mall?"

"Why not?" His eyes twinkled—actually twinkled.

Kirk's irrational whimsy angered her. Was he as snowed as the rest of the world?

"I—"

*"Shh!"* The headphone lady pointed to her equipment, then to Santa Claus, who had risen.

Virginia sat cross-legged before him.

Santa uncurled a parchment paper. "'Twas the night before Christmas...'"

Amanda rolled her eyes. Kirk saw her expression, laughed silently and put his arm around her shoulders. "Now be nice," he whispered, leaning close to her ear.

Oh, it was a wonderful reading, with Santa's stentorian baritone rumbling over them, enthralling the crowd. Was Amanda the only one who recognized the affected accent of a stage actor?

This Santa was a pro. Literally.

And, accompanied by applause, he gave Virginia an exquisite doll wearing a red velvet dress, white fur hat and muff.

*They're bribing her.* That was cheating, wasn't it? But how could she expect a six-year-old to recognize a bribe?

"The stakes have gone up," Kirk murmured.

Amanda itched to say something as Virginia joined them, but that was really the province of her father.

"Look at my doll." Virginia held it up for his inspection.

"Did you remember to thank Santa?" Kirk prompted as he admired the doll.

Santa wanted more than thanks, Amanda knew. Santa wanted to be named "Best Santa of the Mall." It would look great on a résumé.

"Yes, Daddy." Virginia lifted the doll's skirts to check for underwear. "Lace!"

Good grief, the doll wore better underwear than Amanda did.

"Are you ready for another ride in the limousine?" Kirk asked.

"Uh-huh." Virginia held her doll in one hand and clasped her father's hand in the other. "C'mon, Amanda," she said.

Was that it? No lecture on the evils of bribery?

Kirk gave Amanda a warning look and she reluctantly remained silent.

As the three of them walked toward the exit, Amanda caught their reflection in the store windows. A man, a woman and a child—a child who skipped and swung the man's arm.

They looked just like a family.

Amanda stared at the picture they made and noticed Kirk doing the same. He smiled, first at her, then at Virginia, then at Amanda again.

She shivered, feeling uneasy. He was attracted to her, she knew. But was he attracted to Amanda solely for herself—or because she and Virginia had hit it off? What would he feel toward her if he didn't have Virginia to consider?

To her surprise, Amanda discovered that it had become terribly important to clarify Kirk's feelings toward her and her alone. Even more surprising was the realization that her feelings for him had undergone a fundamental shift.

She was falling in love with him and couldn't seem to stop.

Confessing the story of her failed marriage had removed a layer of bitterness that had smothered all prior romantic relationships. It left her free to love again, and love was coming faster than she'd ever imagined it could. She wasn't ready to love again, especially when loving Kirk would mean changing everything about her life.

Late in the afternoon, a local television reporter waylaid them as they waited for Virginia to finish talking with Santa at the last mall they would visit.

Amanda, remembering her days as a reporter scrambling for a quote, indicated that she agreed to be interviewed.

"And we want the dad, too," the woman said, pulling Kirk into camera range.

"What do I do?" Kirk whispered as the reporter began setting up for her introduction.

"Remember to look at her and not the camera," Amanda instructed him. "Keep your answers short and—"

She broke off abruptly as the reporter began speaking.

"—here with Virginia McEnery's parents."

"Oh, no!"

"It's okay," Kirk murmured.

Amanda was torn between correcting the reporter and knowing that to do so would make the woman look bad. Unfortunately they were broadcasting a live remote.

"How did Virginia become a Santa expert?" the reporter asked, and thrust a microphone at Amanda.

"I'm Amanda Donnelly with 'Hello Houston,'" Amanda identified herself. The woman maintained a professional smile, not the slightest glimmer of recognition in her eyes. Miffed, Amanda continued, "We wanted to do a story on children visiting Santa Clauses—"

"And so you started taping your daughter's visits to Santa."

"She's—"

The reporter turned to Kirk. "Has Virginia decided on a favorite Santa Claus yet?"

"She hasn't said," Kirk replied, bending too close to the microphone.

"I heard Virginia's looking for the real Santa Claus. How will she identify him?"

Kirk's brow wrinkled. "She says she has a secret test, but she won't tell us what it is."

"Well, we hope she finds Santa Claus in Dallas." The reporter turned back to the camera, advised viewers to watch Virginia's reports and signed off.

"Wait…" Amanda wanted to correct the woman, but Kirk stopped her.

"Let it go." He nodded toward a small figure. "Here comes one tired little girl."

A drooping Virginia, carrying the world's largest candy cane, trudged toward them. "Can I go home now?"

Kirk grinned and swung her into his arms. "Back to the hotel for you."

Over his shoulder, Virginia beckoned. "Amanda, will you carry this for me, please?"

"Sure." Amanda took the candy cane, mentally tallying up the bribes Virginia had received and hoping they wouldn't interfere with her ratings. "You've done a great job today. Better than some grown-ups I've worked with."

"Yeah?" Virginia rested her head on Kirk's shoulder and grinned.

He kissed her lightly on the temple and hoisted her more firmly against him, murmuring something only Virginia could hear. She nodded and closed her eyes, a smile of contentment on her face.

The sight caused a surprising yank on Amanda's heartstrings. "Yeah," she managed, her voice rough.

# CHAPTER TEN

WHEN HER ALARM BUZZED on Monday morning, Amanda batted it into silence. Without hesitating an instant, she called Kay and told her she wouldn't be in until Virginia's taping later in the afternoon.

Amanda had some thinking to do. Serious thinking. She stared at the ceiling above her bed and thought. And what she thought was that she was becoming too emotionally involved with Kirk and his daughter.

Virginia was like no child Amanda had ever known. Previously children had been an abstract concept to her, something that was not a part of her life or life-style. She'd never considered them as people with opinions and ideas; she either worked with them or avoided them. Actually, she rarely considered them at all. She'd even congratulated herself for coming to the realization that she wasn't destined for motherhood.

And then she'd met Virginia.

And Virginia's father.

And she'd become dissatisfied with her life.

But why? Was this just her normal Christmas blues? Would all be well after the holidays?

She and Kirk had had an unusual courtship, if one could call it a courtship. Too many times in the years since her divorce, she'd engaged in surface dating, investing weeks in someone without ever really knowing him at all. She and Kirk had skipped the surface and had begun on a deeper level than she'd reached with any man since her marriage.

Her marriage. She'd thought she'd known Trenton and she obviously hadn't. The experience made her wary.

But all that had happened nine years ago. Hadn't she grown any in nine years? Hadn't her judgment matured? Just because her feelings for Kirk had developed quickly, did that make them less genuine?

Restless, Amanda threw back the covers. Kirk was right. She engaged in annual pity parties. It was time to grab Christmas back from Trenton.

Several hours later Amanda dragged the last of the shopping bags upstairs to her apartment and carefully dumped them in the middle of her living room.

She'd bought Christmas. And Christmas took up a lot of space. Most of the space. Amanda shoved sacks of ornaments to one side and sat on her couch.

Had she gone berserk? Where was she going to put everything?

On the tree, naturally. Amanda poked the large box containing her brand-new artificial Christmas tree and the magic words "assembly required."

Sighing, she began to assemble.

Half an hour later, she acknowledged that assembling by herself was no fun. She turned on the radio, hoping for Christmas music. For years, she'd avoided Christmas music, which had been nearly impossible. So where was a good carol when you needed one?

By the time she had to leave to pick up Virginia, Amanda felt the Christmas spirit had slipped away. Unfortunately her living room was still covered in Christmas slop.

What had she been thinking? No one would ever see the tree. *She* would barely have time to enjoy it. Maybe Virginia...

Yes, Virginia. Time to go pick her up. With a shake of her head, Amanda grabbed her car keys.

When she and Virginia arrived at the "Hello Houston" studio, there was a message from Kirk's housekeeper asking if Amanda could drive Virginia home after the day's taping. It seemed that Kirk was showing the Rambling Ranch again. Amanda didn't mind. She was curious to see where Kirk and Virginia lived.

Around dinnertime, Amanda found herself parked in front of a two-story contemporary house in West University.

"Is this your house?" she asked Virginia.

"Uh-huh." Virginia nodded. "Want to see my room?"

"Uh-huh." Amanda nodded back. She was desperate to see the inside of Kirk's house. Desperate to learn more about the man who'd turned her life upside down.

From the two-story entry to the block-glass walls, the house was an architectural showplace. Amanda felt as though she'd stepped into a magazine. Did people actually live here?

"Thank you for bringing Virginia home," said a slim bright-eyed woman in her fifties.

"Amanda's come to see my room!"

"How nice." Mrs. Webster gave Amanda a warm smile. "Go hang up your jacket," she reminded Virginia.

As Virginia raced up the stairs, Mrs. Webster turned to Amanda. "Her father called and he's going to be late again. I *must* leave as soon as this batch of cookies comes out of the oven."

"I can stay for a while," Amanda offered quickly, finding that she would rather stay with Virginia than go back to her Christmas-messy apartment.

Mrs. Webster hesitated, obviously considering. "I do have a sitter list—"

"Go ahead and leave," Amanda urged. "We'll be fine."

Mrs. Webster gave an abrupt nod and gestured for Amanda to follow her into the kitchen. "Virginia talks about you all the time," she said in the midst of giving instructions about dinner and checking on the cookies.

Pleased, Amanda couldn't suppress a smile. "We've spent a lot of time together lately."

Mrs. Webster programed the microwave and set green beans inside. "It's been good for her," she said carefully, and darted a glance toward Amanda. "She's lonely at times."

Amanda, with new awareness, realized she was being cautioned. "I think it's been good for me, as well," she admitted, surprised she could do so with a complete stranger.

Virginia, waiting at the bottom of the stairs, hugged Mrs. Webster goodbye and pulled Amanda upstairs.

Amanda didn't know what she'd expected, but it wasn't the painfully neat and pristine room Virginia led her to.

It was all white, like something designed by the Sugar Plum Fairy. Nothing was out of place and there were no toys visible, except for a few white stuffed animals that looked as if they'd never been played with.

"Do you sleep in here?" Amanda asked, looking at the starched eyelet comforter and beribboned pillows.

Virginia nodded.

"Where are your things?" No sign of trinkets or junky giveaways from fast-food restaurants.

"In here." Virginia ran to a cabinet and opened the doors where, with some relief, Amanda saw toys arranged. But they were arranged as if for display. The dolls were dressed and waiting. Books were shelved alphabetically by author. No posters of juvenile heartthrobs.

"It's all so pretty and neat," Amanda complimented her. But it looked like a room no one lived in, certainly not the room of a real flesh-and-blood child.

"Just like the picture," Virginia said.

"Picture?"

Virginia opened her closet door. Taped inside was a photograph from a magazine. Virginia's room was almost an exact duplicate, including the stuffed animals. It was obvious that Kirk had torn out this picture and handed it to a decorator. And for some reason, Virginia believed she had to keep her room exactly as it appeared in the photograph.

"Mrs. Webster left food," Amanda told her. "Are you hungry?"

Grinning, Virginia raced Amanda down the stairs.

After they ate, they watched a Christmas special on television and Amanda tried not to notice how late it was getting.

Then, during a commercial, she bolted upright and stared around her. "Where are all your Christmas decorations?"

"I don't know." Virginia didn't seem concerned.

Christmas Eve was at the end of next week. Shouldn't Kirk have decorated by now? "Are you going to put up decorations?" Amanda questioned her cautiously.

"We've been busy," Virginia said, obviously quoting either Kirk or Mrs. Webster.

"Well, let's go hunt for them and put them up right now." Amanda found she had an irresistible urge to mess up Kirk's house.

Thus, Amanda found herself assembling her second artificial tree of the day. Virginia poked around in boxes and searched for strings of lights all the while singing songs from her Christmas around the World pageant.

Amanda fetched the last of the cookies from the kitchen and she and Virginia polished them off.

Kirk arrived home seconds after the last cookie disappeared into his daughter's mouth.

"What's all this?" he asked, his face visibly brightening when he saw Amanda.

"Amanda and I are making Christmas!" Virginia jumped up and ran to him, dragging a string of lights behind her.

"*Amanda's* making Christmas?" The pleased look he sent Amanda should have struck fear into her heart, but didn't.

Instead, she felt it swell with love, even as she stood in the center of the room, awkwardly clutching a fake tree branch.

Kirk followed Virginia over to the nearly assembled tree. "You're decorating for Christmas," he said, his smile wide.

"I..." Amanda twisted the branch in her hands, bending it at an angle that would never be found in nature. "I just had this strange urge."

"Sounds encouraging," he said, his eyes crinkling at the corners. "Can I help?" He took the branch from her useless fingers, straightened it and handed it back.

"I'm just about done with the tree," Amanda told him, feeling unaccountably shy. "You could give Virginia a hand with the lights."

"They're crooked, Daddy."

Chuckling, Kirk removed his suit jacket and sat on the floor. Virginia shoved the empty cookie plate out of the way and sat next to him.

"Hey!" Kirk retrieved the plate. "What happened to all the cookies?"

Virginia and Amanda looked at each other and broke into giggles. "That's what happens when you're late for dinner," Amanda told him.

He plugged in a string of lights. Three bulbs were burned out. "Thought I was finally about to sell that house. Virginia, can you hand me a package of light bulbs?"

Amanda stuffed in the last tree branch and stepped back. "No sale?"

Shaking his head, he tossed the burned-out bulbs into a box lid. "The couple went to eat and I sat in the office and waited. Then they called and said they'd let me know next week."

"I'm sorry." She knew how much selling the weird house in Memorial meant to him.

"So am I." His smile was totally for the benefit of Virginia, who had been watching him solemnly. "Bring on the next string of lights," he told her.

Virginia wasn't fooled. Her lower lip quivered. "I wish we hadn't eaten all the cookies."

"It's okay," Kirk told her.

"We'll just bake more," Amanda announced. "Mrs. Webster left dough in the refrigerator. By the time you decide where you want the tree and finish checking all the lights, the cookies will be done." Surely it couldn't be that hard to bake cookies.

OKAY, IT WAS HARDER than she thought. How hot should the oven be?

Amanda found a cookbook and flipped through the cookie section, setting the oven to the average temperature she found in the recipes.

She had no idea what kind of cookies they were—only that the dough was pale and Mrs. Webster had sprinkled red and green sugar on top.

Dropping globs of dough on the cookie sheet, Amanda listened to the murmurs of Kirk and Virginia in the next room and felt a peculiar contentment.

She, who had avoided anything that smacked of domesticity, was baking Christmas cookies—or giving it her best shot. She hadn't thought about the studio or Maria Alvarez or her uncompleted projects in hours.

And she was happy.

"Amanda, Amanda!"

Amanda set the oven timer and rushed into the living room.

"Hurry!" Virginia jumped up and down, her hair bow bobbing.

The tree, wearing only lights, stood in front of the window. Kirk was kneeling underneath, attaching an extension cord. "Okay, Virginia, flip the switch."

The room darkened, then the tree burst into light.

"Look!" Virginia shrieked. "Look!" She danced around the tree.

Of all the elaborate displays the little girl had seen, this tree, devoid of ornaments, was the one that excited her.

Tears clogged Amanda's throat.

Kirk came to stand beside her and together they watched Virginia's dance of joy.

"Thanks for being here tonight," he whispered, and stole a quick kiss.

"I wouldn't have missed it," Amanda told him, and meant every word.

Amanda ate dinner with Kirk and Virginia every night that week. And each night, she found it harder and harder to return to her empty apartment.

Especially since she and Kirk managed to steal some time together after Virginia had gone to bed.

Amanda was happy and confused at the same time. How could she have changed so much in such a short time?

She'd lost her edge. Even finally getting the go-ahead on her child-safety story hadn't brought her the intense satisfaction it should have.

Is this what love did? Took away your edge and made you sentimental and goofy?

Virginia's Santa reports continued. If they'd wanted to let her, Virginia could've become a statewide celebrity, but Amanda quietly refused invitations from far-flung cities. She could see that the little girl was getting tired of visiting Santa Claus after Santa Claus, especially when none of them appeared to be the real one.

But soon it would be over. Christmas was at the end of the week, Virginia's Christmas pageant was tomorrow night, and then school would be out for the holidays. This afternoon, Virginia could tape the last three days' worth of introductions and ratings. She'd just have to pick the one most like the "real" Santa.

Virginia had been subdued lately. None of them, not Kirk, Mrs. Webster or Amanda, could find out why. Nor could they guess what secret gift Virginia had asked of each Santa.

Time was running out, Amanda acknowledged as she drove to Virginia's school. Somehow she had to figure out what Virginia wanted and make sure that when the little girl ran down the stairs on Christmas morning, her heart's desire would be beneath the tree.

Approaching the deserted circular drive of Cameron Elementary, Amanda quickly checked her watch. Was she late? Early?

She pulled her car right up to the front doors and waited. No one came out, so she parked and made her way into the school.

At once, she heard the faint strains of a children's choir. Virginia must be rehearsing the Christmas pageant.

Amanda headed for the cafetorium and pushed open the doors, slipping quietly inside. No chairs were set up, so she leaned against the back wall and watched.

All the children were in costumes.

All but one.

Virginia spotted her almost immediately. Sobbing, the little girl ran toward Amanda and flung herself against Amanda's legs.

Mrs. Hull, the principal, sailed over. "Virginia says she doesn't have a costume," the woman murmured in a concerned undertone. "The pageant's tomorrow night."

"I... Did you tell her father?"

"Notes went home with all the children."

"He must not have seen it." Amanda looked down at the sobbing Virginia and remembered that Kirk hadn't even known his daughter was in a pageant until Amanda had told him. She bent down. "Virginia, we'll find something. Don't worry." Straightening, she asked Mrs. Hull, "What's she supposed to be?"

"A little Dutch girl."

"Okay. Wooden shoes. Funky hat. Gotcha. Come on, Virginia."

Virginia's sobs dwindled into sniffles as Amanda dug in her waist pack for some tissues. "Beth's mommy's been sewing hers all week." Virginia looked up at Amanda, eyes full of tears. "But I don't have a mommy."

At that point, Amanda would have promised anything to give Virginia a happily-ever-after ending and would have defied anyone to act differently. She forced herself to answer unemotionally. "No, but you've got me. And *I've* got a whole studio full of costumes."

At the studio Virginia tried racing through her taping, flubbed her lines and declared she didn't remember anything about any of the Santa Clauses.

Kay, who was usually amused by Virginia's antics, left the room after leveling a stern look at Amanda.

At last Virginia successfully finished two Santa ratings. Soon she and Amanda found themselves deep in the bowels of the wardrobe department. "Hello Houston" had broadcast a children's afternoon show for years, and Amanda knew she'd be able to find *something* she could use to put together a costume.

"Holy moly, look at this." Amanda read the tag next to a plastic-shrouded rack of hanging clothes.

"What's it say?" Virginia stood on her tiptoes and looked at the tag. "Christmas—I know that word."

"I know you do, kiddo."

"Christmas a-ro..."

"Around."

"...theee world. Christmas around the World! That's our program!"

"Not exactly," Amanda said, digging out the tags for each plastic bag, "but 'Hello Houston' must have done one like it. Let's see, Alaska—" Amanda flipped through the clothes "—France...Holland. Here you go." She pulled out a heavy bag and hung it on the end of the rack. Unzipping the bag, she peeled it back to find several outfits for both little Dutch girls and little Dutch boys.

"Ooh, ooh!" Virginia tried to pull off the first thing she grabbed.

"Wait a minute," Amanda said. "Let's see if one is your size."

"What about wooden shoes and a hat?"

"They'll be in those white boxes with the labels. Don't just grab—" Virginia had run over to the shelves and begun opening boxes at random.

As it turned out, all the dresses were a little large, but with the judicious use of safety pins, Virginia would be fine.

Her dress was a blue that exactly matched her eyes, and included a white apron and yes, white hat and wooden shoes. Amanda thought Virginia looked wonderful, even if no one had spent a week sewing the costume especially for her.

"I can hardly wait to show Daddy!" Virginia gave a little hop.

"Yeah. I can't wait to talk to him, either," Amanda said, with a grim note that Virginia didn't notice.

It was long past dinnertime when Amanda drove Virginia home.

"I was getting worried," Kirk said, meeting them at the door. A first.

"Amanda got my Christmas costume!" Virginia held up a sack. "These are real wooden shoes!"

"Hey." Kirk obligingly peered inside, but sent a puzzled look toward Amanda. "What are they for?"

"Virginia's playing a little Dutch girl in the Christmas pageant tomorrow night," Amanda said, each word distinct. She didn't smile.

One look at Amanda's face and Kirk sent Virginia upstairs to hang up her costume and wash her hands for dinner. "What happened?" he asked as soon as she was out of earshot.

"I went to pick her up today and stumbled into the dress rehearsal. Virginia didn't have a costume."

"I didn't know she needed a costume."

Remembering Virginia's sobs, Amanda lost her temper. "She's in a Christmas pageant, so of *course* she needs a costume!"

"No one told me."

"You should have known!"

"Well, I didn't!"

Amanda, conscious that their voices were raised, took a breath and tried to rein in her anger. "The principal sent a note home to all the parents."

"I didn't get any note."

"Did you look for one in her school papers?" Honestly.

Kirk rubbed the back of his neck. "Mrs. Webster sorts through those and puts them in the kitchen."

Amanda eyed him shrewdly. "When was the last time you read them?"

He looked away, jaw tightening. "Okay, I blew it." He smiled an apology. "Thanks for bailing me out."

Amanda understood what had happened. She even sympathized with him. But the sound of Virginia's sobbing echoed through her mind and the thought of what might have happened if she hadn't intervened haunted her.

It was essential that Kirk understand. "I was glad to help," she said, adding, "but what if I hadn't been there?"

"Then I suppose someone from the school would have called." His voice held an edge that warned her not to pursue the subject. "That's why they have dress rehearsals—to make sure everyone has a costume."

"So you get a call at the last minute, then what?"

"I would have taken care of it."

"You—or Mrs. Webster? Or somebody from the office?"

Amanda braced herself for an explosion. She should have made sure he understood the importance of a Christmas pageant in the life of a child and left it at that.

But Kirk didn't explode. Shoving his hands into his pockets, he gazed up the stairs toward Virginia's room. "I'm not perfect. I never pretended to be."

Amanda's anger faded. She reached out and touched his arm. "I know it's hard. I also know you've been spending more time with her."

He nodded, returning his gaze to Amanda. "What sort of part does Virginia have?"

"I'm a little fuzzy on the details, but they're doing Christmas around the World and she's a Dutch girl. Oh, you'll have to make tucks in the waist of her skirt with safety pins before she wears it tomorrow night."

"The show's tomorrow night?" Kirk asked sharply, then sighed. "What time?"

Amanda looked at him suspiciously. "I have no idea." Until this afternoon, Amanda hadn't given Virginia's Christmas pageant much thought, except when she had to work around the rehearsals.

"Aren't you going to be there?" Kirk was looking at her as though he'd assumed she would be.

"Well, I hadn't planned on it." Amanda reviewed her schedule. There were a few loose ends to finish before Christmas. "I can try, I suppose."

"Good." He seemed relieved. "I know Virginia would want you there."

"Don't get her hopes up. I've got a lot of work to do." Amanda slung her purse onto her shoulder. "And that means I've got to go back to the studio tonight." She leaned forward and kissed his cheek. It was an I'm-off-to-work kiss. Very domestic—too domestic.

Not at all satisfying.

# CHAPTER ELEVEN

"GUESS WHAT?" Kay walked into Amanda's office, dropped a pile of papers on the floor and hiked herself onto the edge of the desk.

"More Santa Claus stuff?" Amanda asked wearily. She'd spent more time on rating Santa Clauses than on any other story this year.

"Nope, but a present for you."

"I like presents." Amanda tossed her pen onto the desk and stretched her arms over her head. It had been a very late night, and she'd grabbed less than five hours of sleep before returning to the studio this morning. "Well?"

Kay grinned, drawing out the suspense. "Maria Alvarez is going on maternity leave again."

"No!" Amanda's heart kicked into overdrive as possibilities stretched before her. "And I thought she was just getting tubby from too much fruitcake."

"As if you haven't been watching her waist for the last three years."

Amanda couldn't deny it. "I'm...I'm so *happy* for Maria." *Who's going to fill in for her?* Amanda could hardly stand it.

Kay, looking sly, picked up a piece of paper. "Scissors?"

Amanda rooted in her desk drawer until she found a pair. Kay knew something, and Amanda desperately wanted to question her.

"Everything set up for Christmas Eve?" the producer asked, snipping a rectangle from the paper.

Amanda thought she might just scream. "Virginia hasn't decided which Santa is *the* Santa yet, but her Christmas pageant is tonight and school lets out tomorrow for the holidays."

"The earlier she makes her choice the better, as far as publicity goes." Kay took Amanda's nameplate and taped the paper rectangle over the front.

Amanda surrendered to curiosity. "*What* are you doing?"

Kay admired her handiwork. "Amanda Donnelly." She flipped the nameplate toward Amanda. "Producer." The word "associate" had been covered. "Nice sound, eh?"

"Kay—" Amanda tried to slow her breathing "—don't joke."

Kay beamed. "No joke. You are hereby officially promoted to producer."

"Promoted? Not *acting* producer?"

Kay inclined her head.

Amanda Donnelly, producer. It began to sink in. "What about when Maria comes back from maternity leave?"

"She wants to go to part-time status and spend more time with her family." Kay slipped off the desk.

Maria Alvarez, one of Houston's most popular and familiar personalities, wanted to slow down? Amanda had always thought Maria was destined for network television. Taking time off for her family now would weaken her chances.

"Usually I caution my new producers that they'll have to put in more hours," Kay was saying, "but you practically live here as it is. Congratulations, Amanda. You've worked hard.''

Amanda Donnelly, producer. She'd finally just about caught up with Maria Alvarez. Finally caught up to where she would've been if she hadn't wasted time marrying Trenton.

Producer. *Producer*. Her smile muscles hurt.

"Now, sorry to dump this on you before you've celebrated, but I've *got* to have the production figures for the first quarter of next year and—'' Kay edged toward the door "—I need them before Christmas."

"*What?*"

"You'll have to meet with Maria about those."

"Kay, I've still got the Santa story to finish. When's Maria leaving?"

"Tomorrow. She's been ordered to rest." Kay smiled wryly. "Too much job stress."

"Tomorrow?" Amanda sat there with her mouth open. How was she supposed to finish everything in time?

"Did I mention that you'll be moving into Maria's office?"

It was a transparent bribe. But it worked.

By evening, Amanda was nearly cross-eyed. Maria Alvarez had given her sketchy details, but it was up to Amanda to get the reports done and submitted on time, or the stories—including her child-safety piece—wouldn't be funded.

It was a huge responsibility for her first assignment as producer, and Kay knew it. But Kay was counting on her and Amanda wouldn't let her down.

There was someone else she shouldn't let down—Virginia.

It couldn't be helped. Amanda hadn't told Virginia that she'd be at the pageant tonight and now with all this work... Well, Kirk would be there.

For another five minutes, Amanda tried to make sense of production charts, and estimated crew, studio and talent costs.

Kirk *would* be there tonight, wouldn't he? After the costume fiasco, surely he wouldn't forget.

Maybe a quick reminder call was in order. Amanda punched the number of his office. No answer. She rang his house. No answer.

Good.

Or was it good? He and Virginia were on their way to the school, weren't they?

Amanda focused on her schedules. *Estimated number of studio hours...* She hoped Kirk remembered to take safety pins.

After a few more fruitless attempts to work, Amanda gave up. She left a message on her voice mail, grabbed her purse and jacket, found three safety pins and headed for Cameron Elementary.

She needed a break, anyway.

The school was crowded with parents and children. Amanda squeezed into the back of the cafetorium and scanned the crowd for Kirk's dark head.

She didn't see him, but the overheated room was packed. Amanda found a seat in the back and considered herself lucky to do so.

Along the corridor outside the cafetorium, costumed children anxiously craned their necks. Parents with video cameras recorded the event for posterity.

Behind the onstage curtain, youthful faces peered out. Seeing Virginia's taut expression, Amanda stood and waved until the little girl saw her.

Virginia's head disappeared behind the curtain and minutes later, a small hand clutched Amanda's arm. "Where's Daddy? Is he in the bathroom?"

"I just got here," Amanda said, dread settling in her stomach. Kirk had better hurry. "How's your costume? Did someone pin it for you?"

"Mrs. Webster." Virginia stood on a chair and strained to see the doors.

"It looks great." Amanda tried to distract her. "Where's your hat and shoes?"

"Back there."

Amanda assumed she meant behind the stage.

The lights flicked on and off. A parental murmur vibrated through the audience and a stern-faced teacher hissed at Virginia.

"Make him hurry, Amanda! We're almost going to start!" Virginia called as she ran toward the stage in her stocking feet.

Amanda spent as much time watching the doors to the cafetorium as she did the performances on stage. Country after country paraded past.

When it was time for Holland, Virginia, standing apart from the singing group, said a piece about the Christmas customs in that country. She looked adorable, and Amanda felt an unexpected pride.

When the program was over and the lights came back on, Amanda tried to find Kirk one last time before admitting it was futile.

Unbelievably, he'd missed his daughter's Christmas program. After the costume crisis, after their discussion, how *could* he? He'd better have a *real* good reason.

Amanda waited to congratulate Virginia and kept an eye out for Mrs. Webster.

The student performers had returned to their class-rooms where their parents would meet them. Amanda finally found a tight-lipped Virginia sitting at her desk and staring straight ahead. Her wooden shoes were in her lap.

Amanda took one look at the families swirling around the quiet girl and nearly succumbed to a mix of helplessness and compassion. Something terrible must have happened to Kirk. But for Virginia's sake—and her own—she had to hide her fears.

"Hey, there's the star!" Amanda swooped in, trying to create some of the excitement the other children were experiencing.

Virginia's smile wavered and disappeared. She obviously wasn't fooled.

"You were great tonight. And you had the best costume."

"Thank you for lending it to me," Virginia said politely, sounding far too old for a child of six.

Searching for something—*anything*—to say, Amanda picked up the wooden shoes. "They're not at all comfortable, are they?"

Virginia shook her head.

The last of the children and their parents were leaving. The teacher raised her eyebrows at Amanda.

"Where's Mrs. Webster?" Amanda asked, not seeing any sign of the housekeeper.

"I don't know." Virginia shrugged. "She dropped me off."

*How was Virginia supposed to get home?*

"My daddy didn't come, did he?"

What could Amanda say? "I know he wanted to." But she didn't know that at all. Once again, helplessness nearly overwhelmed her. She wanted to break something. Or somebody.

Instead, she bent and hugged a stiff Virginia. "Let's go home."

Neither Amanda nor Virginia said anything during the drive. Amanda wanted to offer words of comfort, but felt too inadequate.

Kirk met them at the front door, still dressed in his suit. "How was the pageant?"

Amanda let all her frustration, anger and anxiety show on her face and gestured to Virginia.

Kirk got the message. For endless moments, he met Amanda's eyes, his own pleading for understanding.

All right, she'd listen to his explanation. It'd better be a humdinger.

A solemn Kirk knelt in front of Virginia, taking her hands in his. "I'm sorry I wasn't there. I *wanted* to be there."

"That's what Amanda said."

"And Amanda's right." He smiled up at her. "But I couldn't get away. You know that house I've been trying to sell?"

Virginia nodded.

"Well, tonight, some people decided to buy it. Only, they offered to pay less than the owners were asking, so I had to call the owners and see if they would sell their house, anyway. Unfortunately all the owners don't live in the same city and by the time I could talk to them, it was time for your pageant to start."

"Didn't you tell them about my pageant?"

Kirk dipped his head and squeezed Virginia's arms. Breathing deeply, he met her gaze once more. "No, honey, I didn't."

Virginia's eyes welled with tears.

So did Amanda's.

Groaning, Kirk enfolded the little girl in his arms as Amanda looked away. She knew he felt guilty right now. She knew how much he wanted to sell that kooky house. But still.

"I'm so sorry. You know I wanted to be there, don't you?"

Virginia nodded. "I understand." Her face pressed to his shoulder. "I love you, Daddy."

Way to go, Virginia. Twist that knife.

Feeling like an intruder, Amanda left the hallway and stood by the Christmas tree. Kirk found her there several minutes later.

"Virginia?" she asked.

"Getting ready for bed."

Amanda exhaled. Virginia was a lot more forgiving than she was.

"We're going to have an argument now, aren't we?"

"You betcha."

"Will it save time if I tell you I feel lousy about missing her pageant?"

"That's promising."

"Amanda, I know it looks bad, but will you listen?"

Taking her silence for assent, he continued, "I finally got a bid on the Rambling Ranch."

"Congratulations. Where's the champagne?"

"Still corked."

Amanda looked at him accusingly. "You mean after all this you didn't get the sale?"

"Not yet," Kirk said grimly. "The buyers were sitting in my office with their bid—and it's a good one, though not what the sellers wanted. The thing is, the house has lost value and it's been standing empty. The owners haven't seen it in a couple of years and don't know its condition. Anyway, I tried to set up a conference call between them. It just took too long."

Amanda gazed at the tree, remembering the night they decorated it, remembering the feelings she'd shared with Kirk. Wondering how she could be so angry with him now. "So what happened?"

"The house is owned by two brothers and a sister. The sister wasn't home."

Amanda glanced over her shoulder, then back at the tree. "Probably at her child's Christmas pageant."

He sighed. "Look, I'm sorry I wasn't there, but this is not the end of the world. Sometimes things don't go the way we want them to. Virginia needs to know that."

"Oh, she knows it all right."

"Amanda..." She could hear the frustration in his voice. Good. "There'll be other pageants."

"There'll be other houses," she shot back.

"Not this one. You know what selling this house means to me."

"And you should've known what that Christmas pageant meant to Virginia. How can you expect her to understand? She's only in the first grade, and the room was loaded with other parents and grandparents. She had a featured part!"

"She did?" He winced.

*"Yes,"* Amanda answered. "And she wanted you to be there. It was awful. She looked and looked. It broke my heart."

"I'm glad you were able to make it." His voice was gruff.

"Which is something else—what if I hadn't been there? How was she supposed to get home? Mrs. Webster just dropped her off."

His mouth worked before he admitted, "When I knew I wouldn't be able to get away, I called your office. The message said you'd gone to the school."

"So you just *assumed* I'd know to bring her home?" Amanda stared at him in disbelief.

"I figured you'd realize I wasn't there and..." He trailed off at Amanda's expression.

What if she hadn't sought out Virginia? The thought of the little girl's waiting until someone realized she was missing made Amanda feel sick.

"I shouldn't have done that." Kirk ran his hand over the back of his neck. "All I could think about was that I might finally sell that house."

"But Kirk, ever since I've known you, you've depended on others to pick up Virginia when you run late, drive her places if you're with a client, or rearrange their schedule at a moment's notice to accommodate you. It's got to stop."

"I know." He reached for her arm, drawing her toward him. "You can see how much I need you. How much *we* need you."

"I don't want to be needed!" she declared, surprising them both. Kirk released her arm. "If you're only looking for somebody to take care of Virginia, then count me out."

He looked stunned. "I've made no secret of my feelings for you. In fact, I—"

"Don't." Amanda held up her hand. If he told her he loved her now, she'd never say what had to be said. "I went to that program tonight because I had this awful feeling you wouldn't be there. You knew I'd go—you were banking on it."

"I explained what happened." Anger tinged his words.

"Did it once occur to you that *I* might have job responsibilities tonight?"

"Then you shouldn't have gone," he answered reasonably.

Amanda didn't feel like being reasonable. "*Somebody* had to. It should have been you."

"In an ideal world it would have been." Kirk looked away. "In an ideal world Virginia would have two parents. But this isn't an ideal world, so I cope the best I can." Amanda heard the pain in his voice and felt like a heel.

"I'm sorry. Raising a child must be a tremendous undertaking. I have no idea what it's like."

There was a deep silence. "That frightens you, doesn't it?" Kirk asked perceptively. "You're becoming more and more involved with us and you're scared."

She had to make him understand. Understand that she realized how much Virginia needed a mother. And realized that she wasn't going to be good enough. "I'm not scared. I'm realistic. Once you're no longer a single father, people will expect you to take care of Virginia yourself. And I think that your...your..."

"Wife?"

Amanda swallowed. "That your wife will end up doing everything."

He regarded her in the twinkling light of the Christmas tree. "I'd expect my wife to help raise Virginia, yes. I would hope that she'd want to because she cared for her."

But what about his wife's job? Would it always take second place to Kirk's? Amanda straightened her shoulders. "I got a promotion today. I've been a full producer for—" she squinted at her watch "—nine hours now."

"Hey, that's great."

"Thanks." She could tell he was genuinely happy for her. But did he understand all the job entailed? "It's what I've worked toward ever since my divorce. The hours are long and there's a lot of stress, but I'm looking forward to the challenge."

His smile faded. "Is this your way of telling me you'll be busy the next time I call?"

She had to be honest. "Very likely. I shouldn't even be here now. I was working on production budgets that are due before Christmas, and I've got to get back to the studio." Her fingers sought the solace of her worry stone. "I don't know how I'm going to get everything done."

Kirk touched her cheek, forcing her to meet his eyes. "And this is what you want?"

"What do you mean?"

"No life outside that television studio?"

"It's the life I chose and I love it." At least, she *had* loved it.

"No responsibilities toward anyone but yourself, right?"

She knew where he was headed. "I won't have *time* to take on other responsibilities."

"Meaning Virginia and me."

"Meaning I've worked nine years toward this. And whether you realize it or not, you need a stay-at-home wife."

"If you're worried that I'll ask you to quit your job—"

"No," Amanda interrupted, because she knew he never would. "I'm worried that I'll want to."

Raising a finger, he traced the line of her jaw. "And would that be so bad?"

"I can't do it," she whispered. "I gave up everything once..." Amanda almost broke down. "Find somebody better for Virginia. Somebody who'll run the car pool and bake brownies and be president of the PTA. Somebody who'll sit front row center at every Christmas pageant."

"What about somebody for me?" Kirk asked, holding her close.

Amanda pushed away. "I c-can't be that person."

"Without even trying?"

Trying would only lead to a deeper hurt. "It wouldn't work."

"You sound very sure," he said, his voice flat.

"I am."

She thought he might protest, but he didn't. "It's just as well that the last of the Santa broadcasts is on Christmas Eve. Then you won't have any reason to see us again, will you?"

"I guess not." Amanda could barely choke out the words.

"I think a clean break would be best. It will be easier for me to explain to Virginia why—"

An unearthly wailing came from the stairs.

"Virginia!" Kirk bolted toward her, Amanda right behind.

The sobbing girl clung to the railing halfway down the steps. Kirk pried her fingers loose and gathered her into his arms.

She'd overheard them.

After everything else, listening to her cry and to Kirk's soothing murmurs was too much.

Amanda felt like an emotional zombie. She approached the stairs and found the heap of blue and white at the bottom. Virginia's costume. Stiffly, Amanda bent to pick it up, meeting Kirk's eyes as she stood.

He gazed at her, his expression cold. "I think you'd better go."

# CHAPTER TWELVE

"THERE IS NO Santa Claus." Virginia sat on a stool in front of the camera and refused to say anything else. Studio time was ticking away. In a few moments, another show was scheduled to be taped.

Amanda leaned her head against the wall. Ever since Mrs. Webster had brought her to the studio, Virginia had stubbornly refused to cooperate.

"Virginia?" Amanda approached her.

Glacial blue eyes swiveled toward her, then away.

"Honey, you have to choose the best Santa Claus. Tomorrow's Christmas Eve."

"No. They're all fake."

"Is there one you thought was a pretty good fake?"

Virginia shook her head.

"Would you like to look at all the videotapes? Maybe that'll help you remember."

"Don't need to. They all flunked my test."

Amanda grabbed hold of her evaporating patience. She knew she was to blame for Virginia's recalcitrance. "What was your test?"

"To give me my Christmas wish."

"What was your wish?"

Virginia shook her head. "Santa will know."

Amanda closed her eyes in frustration. When she opened them, she saw Kay, who gave her the hurry-up signal from the control booth. "If you won't tell me, will you tell Kay?"

"No."

"Ron?"

"No."

"Mrs. Webster?"

Virginia shook her head.

"Your dad?" Amanda had avoided thinking about Kirk. Tossing him back into the matrimonial pond had been the hardest thing she'd ever done. Maybe some day, when Virginia had children of her own, she'd finally appreciate what Amanda had done for her.

"Daddy knows."

*What?* And he hadn't told her?

Sighing, she beckoned to Mrs. Webster, who was observing from behind a glass partition. "Why don't you take Virginia on home? If she thaws, let me know."

Mrs. Webster gave her a frosty nod. Great. Everyone hated her.

"Amanda." Kay wandered out of the control booth. "Far be it from me to tell you how to do your brand-new job, but we've got to alert the mall where we'll be broadcasting. They'll want to maximize the publicity opportunities. We've been hyping this for days."

"I know, Kay." Amanda had both hands in her pockets. She rubbed her worry stones so hard she thought the heat would scorch the fabric.

"What's wrong with the kid?"

"She's a lonely little girl and she…got too attached to me."

Kay twirled the headphones she held. Just before putting them back on she said, "Sounds like you two were a good match."

Back in her office—she hadn't had time to move to Maria's more spacious one—Amanda tried to schedule studio time for the next calendar quarter. She'd done it before and it'd always worked out. But before, it was just something she submitted with her pitches—something extra to save the producer time.

Apparently no one else was gunning for producer.

Giving up, she admitted she'd be unable to concentrate until she talked with Kirk.

Kirk wasn't in his office.

"We've got our fingers crossed," Rosalie confided to her. Obviously Rosalie was unaware of Amanda's pariah status. "The Rambling Ranch owners are flying in today. It'll be *so* great for business if we sell that house!"

"Tell him I said good luck. Also, could you leave him a message?"

"Sure."

"Tell him . . . tell him that he knows what Virginia's Christmas wish is and . . . and that he'll have to play Santa."

Rosalie chuckled. "She's a sweetie, isn't she?"

"Yes." Amanda struggled to disguise the emotion in her voice.

"We're all going to be watching tomorrow afternoon."

Swell.

"If I don't talk to you before then, Merry Christmas!"

"Merry Christmas," Amanda echoed.

IT WAS THE WEE HOURS of the morning when Amanda stumbled—literally—through her living room.

Her floor was still littered with Christmas ornaments, boxes, sacks and a nearly assembled Christmas tree. She caught her foot on a box, and when she tried to catch her balance, stepped squarely into a box of glass ornaments.

They crunched.

Why had she bothered? The only time she'd have to decorate would be Christmas Day.

It looked like she'd have lots of time to herself then, even if she ended up doing what she always did on major religious holidays—volunteering for studio duty so somebody with a family could stay home.

Kirk hadn't called. Even though they'd parted in such a miserable way, she'd expected him to return her call.

Reaching for the lamp, she flipped on the light to see what ones had broken. Wasn't there some law that said they would be the most expensive ornaments she'd purchased?

Or the ones with the most sentimental value.

Amanda crouched down and lifted a box full of smashed Santa Clauses.


"THEY'RE ALL FAKE and I'll tell 'em so!"

Amanda stood in the parking lot of the "Hello Houston" studio. Virginia sat in Mrs. Webster's car and refused to come out.

The "Hello Houston" van was packed and ready to go. Amanda just didn't know where to send it.

Kay smoked the first cigarette Amanda had seen her smoke in months.

Whirling on her heel, Amanda ran back into the building. She commandeered the security guard's telephone and called McEnery Realtors.

"McEn—"

"Rosalie, I've got to talk to Kirk right now. Beep him or call him or send out the National Guard."

"Is Virginia injured?"

"Not yet."

"That's the only circumstance under which I can disturb him."

Ah, so Rosalie had been informed of Amanda's change of status to persona non grata. "Rosalie, I'm desperate. Desperate! We go live in two hours and Virginia won't choose a Santa Claus. Now, if she has to bleed before you'll call her father, then I can arrange it."

She must have sounded convincing, because Rosalie put her on hold. Good. She'd explain to Kirk and get him to convince Virginia to cooperate. Then—

"Ms. Donnelly? I'm sorry. Mr. McEnery is unavailable."

Stunned, Amanda returned the telephone to the security guard.

She walked outside and faced the blank faces of the crew. Kay sat in the front seat of the van and puffed cigarette after cigarette. Any moment, she'd take over and Amanda's authority would be forever undermined.

Amanda was the producer. She needed to produce.

Jogging to the van, she announced, "Virginia gave the Buffalo Bayou Santa the highest rating of any Santa so far. We'll go there."

"Let's move," Kay said, grinding out her cigarette.

Ecstatic Buffalo Bayou Mall officials were waiting to greet them. Though, as one confided to Amanda, they'd hired a team of Santas and had to check their employment records to see which one had been on duty the day Virginia had visited. Nevertheless, they were working on it and were thrilled with the honor.

Amanda could hardly speak. Her first live remote as full producer and she had no idea what Virginia would do.

How ironic that the little girl had frequently nailed her lines on the first run-through when they'd been taping and now she refused to discuss any script at all.

And it was live. What if she threw a tantrum? What if she declared the Santa was a fake?

The negative publicity would be horrendous.

"Kay—" Amanda approached the executive producer "—I don't want to go live. Let's tape her and splice the old rating footage into the program."

Kay removed her headphones. "Not take chances? That's not the Amanda Donnelly I know."

Oh, yes it was. She wanted safe and predictable. Boring. Actually, boring was quite attractive.

"You've got first-time jitters," Kay said, replacing her headphones. "Don't worry."

Amanda had done live remotes before and Kay knew it.

"Ms. Donnelly?"

Amanda turned to the mall official.

"We've located the Santa Claus. He'll be here within the hour."

With a sinking feeling, Amanda checked her watch. Great. He'd arrive half an hour before airtime, leaving them no choice but to go live.

After checking with her crew and finding everything under control, Amanda wandered to the toy store where she'd sent Virginia and Mrs. Webster, hoping that Mrs. Webster could divine Virginia's heart's desire.

Amanda spotted them through the window. Virginia looked like a robot. A desperately unhappy robot.

And Amanda realized she felt exactly the same way.

Virginia needed a full-time, brownie-baking mom. Amanda knew that, but apparently Kirk and Virginia didn't.

Why did doing the right thing have to hurt so much?

"WHERE'S SANTA?"

"Changing."

"We're live in seven minutes."

"He won't have time for makeup."

"Is the talent ready?"

"She needs blush."

"Six minutes, Ms. Donnelly."

"Get that cable out of the frame!"

"Ron, pan the mall. Somebody verify the correct spelling of the mall guy's name..."

"Keep the crowd back."

"Sound check!"

"Give me a number-two spot on Santa's throne."

"Hey—what's Santa's name?"

Wearily, Amanda looked at her production assistant. "Santa Claus."

"Oh, right."

Arms crossed mutinously, Virginia stood by the empty gold and red throne. At least she was wearing her candy-cane sweatshirt.

"How are you doing, Virginia?" Amanda asked.

"Horrible."

"It'll all be over in a few minutes. We'd like you to sit on Santa's lap and give your last Santa report, just the way you always do, but this time, tell all the boys and girls that you've decided the Buffalo Bayou Santa is the best Santa you've found."

Virginia's lower lip stuck out.

"Will you do that for me, honey?" Amanda pleaded. "I'm not asking you to say he's the real Santa, just the best one you found."

"Okay." Virginia spoke so softly Amanda could barely hear her.

Relief flooded through her. "Thanks."

"Amanda! Credits are rolling."

Amanda gave a thumbs-up to Virginia and scampered out of camera range. In minutes, "Hello Houston" would cut to them.

*Where was Santa?*

"Where's your Santa?" she demanded of the mall official. "We need him now!"

He shrugged.

She was going to be sick, right here on live television.

Helplessly, she watched the time tick away until she had to cue Virginia.

"Merry Christmas!" chirped Virginia.

Bless her heart. The sparkle was gone, but with all the activity and excitement, probably no one noticed but Amanda.

What everyone did notice was that Santa's throne was conspicuously empty.

Virginia had just started speaking when a faint but extremely welcome, "Ho-ho-ho...Me-e-erry Christmas," became audible.

The crowd parted and Santa arrived in a swirl of artificial snow.

Amanda sat down. She was getting too old for all this stress.

Virginia stood, transfixed, as Santa took his place on the throne and beckoned to her. She took a few steps, stopped and stared.

Santa looked thinner than Amanda remembered, but she'd seen so many....

Giggling, Virginia climbed onto Santa's lap and gave him a hug. "He's the best Santa of them all!" she said.

Amanda was not one to look a gift miracle in the mouth. As the camera focused on a bubbling Virginia, the program finished with a voice-over of the mall official inviting all children to come and visit Santa during Buffalo Bayou Mall's extended holiday shopping hours.

As soon as they were off the air, Amanda ran over to Virginia and Santa Claus.

"That was too close," she said, "but I appreciate you..." She trailed off as Santa tugged down his beard, revealing a familiar face.

Kirk.

"What are you *doing* here?"

"You told me I had to play Santa," he explained, grinning.

"I meant..." But she couldn't finish in front of Virginia.

"Come sit." He patted his lap and Virginia moved over.

"Oh, no, I'm too heavy!"

Kirk grabbed Amanda around the waist and positioned her on his lap. "Kirk!"

Virginia giggled. "Tell her, Daddy, tell her."

"As we speak, ownership of the Rambling Ranch is changing hands."

"You mean, right now?"

Kirk nodded.

"And you're not there?"

Kirk put his arms around them. "No. I'd rather be here with you two."

"But you've been trying to sell that house for so long!" Tears stung Amanda's eyes as she understood the gesture he'd made.

"I used to think it was important that I be there. But when they scheduled the closing for three o'clock today,

I told them no thanks, my daughter was going to be on television and I was going to watch her.''

Amanda knew he was telling her—showing her—that he could change. "You had a great view, too.''

"I would have missed it if it hadn't been for you.'' He turned to Virginia. "Young lady, I believe you had a Christmas wish?''

Virginia's eyes darted from her father to Amanda and she nodded, but said nothing.

"I know *I've* got a Christmas wish,'' Kirk said, the light tone belying the intensity of his expression. "Now tell Santa *your* Christmas wish, Amanda.''

She looked into his eyes, forgetting about all the people and cameras, and said what was in her heart. "I want to be part of your lives. I want us to be a family.''

"That's my wish! That's my wish!'' shrieked Virginia.

"Is that what she's been asking the Santas for?''

Kirk nodded.

"Oh, Virginia,'' Amanda said as the little girl squeezed her hard. "I don't know how to be a mommy. I'll make mistakes, and my job—''

"The important thing,'' Kirk interrupted, tilting Amanda's face so she'd look at him, "is that you're willing to try. And that means I get my wish.'' He kissed her. "I love you.''

"I'm gonna get a mom-my, I'm gonna get a mom-my,'' Virginia sang, and slid off her father's knee.

"I love you,'' Amanda said, smiling at Kirk through her tears. "Both of you.''

She was vaguely aware of applause, and then, with Virginia hopping up and down, Amanda Donnelly kissed Santa Claus.

"Uh, Kay?" Ron pointed to the viewfinder on his camera. "Shouldn't I pan the mall or something? We're going live in fifteen seconds."

"Nah." Kay grinned. "This'll be great for the closing credits."

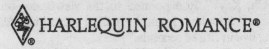

# HARLEQUIN ROMANCE®

### *brings you*

*More Romances Celebrating Love, Families and Children!*

We promised in December, after bringing you
**The Nutcracker Prince** and **The Santa Sleuth**,
that we would have more wonderful titles in our
KIDS & KISSES series. True to our promise, in January
we have the wonderfully warm story **No Ties**
(Harlequin Romance #3344) by Rosemary Gibson. When
Cassie goes to work for Professor Adam Merrick, she finds
not only love and marriage, but a ready-made family!

Watch for more of these special romances from favorite
Harlequin Romance authors in the coming months:

| | | | |
|---|---|---|---|
| February | #3347 | A Valentine for Daisy | Betty Neels |
| March | #3351 | Leonie's Luck | Emma Goldrick |
| April | #3357 | The Baby Business | Rebecca Winters |
| May | #3359 | Bachelor's Family | Jessica Steele |

Available wherever Harlequin books are sold.

This January, Harlequin and Silhouette
proudly bring you

*by Request™*

*Stranded!*

When you're stranded, should you trust your head or
your heart?

Three complete novels by your favorite authors—in
one special collection!

**THE SILVER SNARE** by Stephanie James
**FLASHPOINT** by Patricia Gardner Evans
**A STRANGER'S SMILE** by Kathleen Korbel

Trapped alone with a stranger...the perfect place for
suspicion, tension *and* romance!

Available wherever
Harlequin and Silhouette books are sold.

HARLEQUIN® ▼ *Silhouette*®

 HARLEQUIN®

The proprietors of Weddings, Inc. hope you
have enjoyed visiting Eternity, Massachusetts.
And if you missed any of the exciting Weddings,
Inc. titles, here is your opportunity to complete
your collection:

| Harlequin Superromance | #598 | *Wedding Invitation* by Marisa Carroll | $3.50 U.S. ☐ $3.99 CAN. ☐ |
|---|---|---|---|
| Harlequin Romance | #3319 | *Expectations* by Shannon Waverly | $2.99 U.S. ☐ $3.50 CAN. ☐ |
| Harlequin Temptation | #502 | *Wedding Song* by Vicki Lewis Thompson | $2.99 U.S. ☐ $3.50 CAN. ☐ |
| Harlequin American Romance | #549 | *The Wedding Gamble* by Muriel Jensen | $3.50 U.S. ☐ $3.99 CAN. ☐ |
| Harlequin Presents | #1692 | *The Vengeful Groom* by Sara Wood | $2.99 U.S. ☐ $3.50 CAN. ☐ |
| Harlequin Intrigue | #298 | *Edge of Eternity* by Jasmine Cresswell | $2.99 U.S. ☐ $3.50 CAN. ☐ |
| Harlequin Historical | #248 | *Vows* by Margaret Moore | $3.99 U.S. ☐ $4.50 CAN. ☐ |

## HARLEQUIN BOOKS...
### NOT THE SAME OLD STORY

| | |
|---|---|
| **TOTAL AMOUNT** | $ |
| **POSTAGE & HANDLING** ($1.00 for one book, 50¢ for each additional) | $ |
| **APPLICABLE TAXES*** | $ _____ |
| **TOTAL PAYABLE** (check or money order—please do not send cash) | $ _____ |

To order, complete this form and send it, along with a check or money order for the
total above, payable to Harlequin Books, to: **In the U.S.:** 3010 Walden Avenue,
P.O. Box 9047, Buffalo, NY 14269-9047; **In Canada:** P.O. Box 613, Fort Erie, Ontario,
L2A 5X3.

Name: _____

Address: _____ City: _____

State/Prov.: _____ Zip/Postal Code: _____

*New York residents remit applicable sales taxes.
Canadian residents remit applicable GST and provincial taxes.

WED-F

This holiday, join four hunky heroes under the mistletoe for

# Christmas Kisses

Cuddle under a fluffy quilt, with a cup of hot chocolate and these romances sure to warm you up:

### #561 HE'S A REBEL (also a Studs title)
Linda Randall Wisdom

### #562 THE BABY AND THE BODYGUARD
Jule McBride

### #563 THE GIFT-WRAPPED GROOM
M.J. Rodgers

### #564 A TIMELESS CHRISTMAS
Pat Chandler

Celebrate the season with all four holiday books sealed with a Christmas kiss—coming to you in December, only from Harlequin American Romance!

# CHRISTMAS STALKINGS

All wrapped up in spine-tingling packages, here are three books guaranteed to chill your spine...and warm your hearts this holiday season!

**#302 THE KID WHO STOLE CHRISTMAS**
Linda Stevens

**#303 I'LL BE HOME FOR CHRISTMAS**
Dawn Stewardson

**#304 BEARING GIFTS**
Aimée Thurlo

This December, fill your stockings with the "Christmas Stalkings"—for the best in romantic suspense. Only from

HARLEQUIN®

INTRIGUE®

On the most romantic day of the year, capture the thrill of falling in love all over again—with

## Harlequin's

## Valentine
## Bachelors

They're three sexy and *very single* men who run very special personal ads to find the women of their fantasies by Valentine's Day. These exciting, passion-filled stories are written by bestselling Harlequin authors.

*Your Heart's Desire* by Elise Title
*Mr. Romance* by Pamela Bauer
*Sleepless in St. Louis* by Tiffany White

Be sure not to miss Harlequin's Valentine Bachelors, available in February wherever Harlequin books are sold.

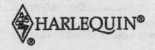

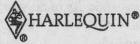

**HARLEQUIN®**

Don't miss these Harlequin favorites by some of our most distinguished authors!
And now you can receive a discount by ordering two or more titles!

| | | | |
|---|---|---|---|
| HT#25483 | BABYCAKES by Glenda Sanders | $2.99 | ☐ |
| HT#25559 | JUST ANOTHER PRETTY FACE by Candace Schuler | $2.99 | ☐ |
| HP#11608 | SUMMER STORMS by Emma Goldrick | $2.99 | ☐ |
| HP#11632 | THE SHINING OF LOVE by Emma Darcy | $2.99 | ☐ |
| HR#03265 | HERO ON THE LOOSE by Rebecca Winters | $2.89 | ☐ |
| HR#03268 | THE BAD PENNY by Susan Fox | $2.99 | ☐ |
| HS#70532 | TOUCH THE DAWN by Karen Young | $3.39 | ☐ |
| HS#70576 | ANGELS IN THE LIGHT by Margot Dalton | $3.50 | ☐ |
| HI#22249 | MUSIC OF THE MIST by Laura Pender | $2.99 | ☐ |
| HI#22267 | CUTTING EDGE by Caroline Burnes | $2.99 | ☐ |
| HAR#16489 | DADDY'S LITTLE DIVIDEND by Elda Minger | $3.50 | ☐ |
| HAR#16525 | CINDERMAN by Anne Stuart | $3.50 | ☐ |
| HH#28801 | PROVIDENCE by Miranda Jarrett | $3.99 | ☐ |
| HH#28775 | A WARRIOR'S QUEST by Margaret Moore | $3.99 | ☐ |

(limited quantities available on certain titles)

| | |
|---|---|
| **TOTAL AMOUNT** | $ |
| **DEDUCT: 10% DISCOUNT FOR 2+ BOOKS** | $ |
| **POSTAGE & HANDLING** | $ |
| ($1.00 for one book, 50¢ for each additional) | |
| **APPLICABLE TAXES*** | $ |
| **TOTAL PAYABLE** | $ |
| (check or money order—please do not send cash) | |

To order, complete this form and send it, along with a check or money order for the total above, payable to Harlequin Books, to: **In the U.S.:** 3010 Walden Avenue, P.O. Box 9047, Buffalo, NY 14269-9047; **In Canada:** P.O. Box 613, Fort Erie, Ontario, L2A 5X3.

Name: _____

Address:_____City: _____

State/Prov.: _____ Zip/Postal Code: _____

*New York residents remit applicable sales taxes.
  Canadian residents remit applicable GST and provincial taxes.

HBACK-OD